THE
MAGIC GARDEN

OF

MY BOOK HOUSE

EDITED BY

OLIVE BEAUPRÉ MILLER

PUBLISHERS

THE BOOK HOUSE for CHILDREN

LAKE BLUFF, ILL.

PREFACE

"THE MAGIC GARDEN" continues with boys and girls in the period of wonder tales. And as the folk tales used in this book and throughout the various volumes come from many different countries, it is interesting to note here some remarkable facts about folk tales in general.

Each race has its own collection of household tales, the germ of which often goes back far beyond the dawn of history. On page 84 of "The Magic Garden" we have the first-known Cinderella story, the Egyptian tale of "Rhodopis and Her Gilded Sandals," which was told to children more than a thousand years before Christ. Like "Cinderella," this story tells of a maiden's lost slipper, how it was used by a prince to discover the identity of his beloved and how all the maidens in the kingdom tried to get their feet into it while it would fit the beloved alone.

One of the most remarkable facts about folk tales is that in countries separated by the widest stretches of land and sea, there are often incidents, plots and characters common to all the tales. Cinderella, or her prototype of the ancient slipper tale, finally developed into the story of the ill-treated but ultimately successful younger daughter, which appears in the folklore of many different peoples. In Volume Six you will find "Pigling and Her Proud Sister," a Korean Cinderella story; and "The Twelve Months," a Czech version of that same tale. Our own Cinderella (Volume Four, page 12), a story told over and over again by English speaking people, actually came to us from France where Charles Perrault, having heard the tale from his nurse in childhood, wrote it down in 1699. It was not translated into English until 1729.

And as widespread as the story of the victorious younger daughter is the story of the victorious younger son who was always called either just plain Jack or Boots, for as Cinderella had to serve her older sisters and do the disagreeable jobs in the household, this younger son had to clean boots for his father and elder brothers. He is always despised by these elder brothers and yet succeeds at various difficult tasks where the elders fail. Such stories are "Boots and His Brothers," from the Norse; "How Jack Sought the Golden Apples," from the English, both to be found in Volume Five; "The Princess on the Glass Hill," from the Norse, "Chylde Roland and the Goblin King," from the English and "The Good Comrades of the Flying Ship," from the Russian, all of which are in Volume Six. And here in Volume Seven we have the very same character in "The Golden Bird," from the German and "The Prince Who Rode Through a Mousehole," from the Czech.

There are many other themes common to the lore of widely separated races and we can scarcely suppose that the similarity of these stories is to be explained by conscious borrowing, since the common people, the peasants, who are the guardians of the ancient store of legends in every land, have in the past read little and traveled less. It is possible that in the dim beginnings of history when the Aryan race still lived as a single people, they already possessed many of these stories and when they scattered to lands as far distant from each other as Ceylon and Iceland they bore with them the germ at least of many of their household tales. But the most probable explanation seems to be that the similarity in these tales is due to the similarity of primitive man's imagination, intellect and emotions everywhere, no matter how separated by material barriers. No one thing gives a better conception of the universal oneness of human nature than a glance over its old folk tales. Thus, stories of the despised younger son or daughter, who finally succeeds, seem to express humanity's everlasting sympathy with the underdog.

In addition to folk tales in "The Magic Garden" we have some wonder tales from classic Greek myths, such as the story of "Phaeton" and "The Golden Touch," as told by Nathaniel Hawthorne. Furthermore, we have, related in fantasy to these tales, the story of "Columbine and Her Playfellows," as it has delighted both adults and children for generations in presentations of the Italian pantomime, and the story of "Punch and Judy," the ancient and famous puppets, who have made people laugh for as many generations.

Again Shakespeare is with us here in "The Winter's Tale." And we have one of the most adventurous stories from the Bible, the story of David from his boyhood, through his slaying of Goliath, his flight from Saul and his life as the leader of a band of men in the wilderness, up to the time when he became king.

On the side of the realistic tale, put in for balance to offset the highly imaginative stories, is the story of David Copperfield's adventure when he went to the seashore with Peggotty to visit her brother's family who lived in the strange old boat turned into a house. This story was taken from the novel, "David Copperfield," by Charles Dickens. Already in Volume Six the child has met Dickens through "Little Nell and Mrs. Jarley's Wax-Work," so we still progress in giving the child an association with the greatest authors in English literature.

CONTENTS

THE MAGIC GARDEN

Miska and the Man-With-The-Iron-Head
A Hungarian Fairy Tale

Once upon a time there lived in a little hut in Hungary a very poor family and when the oldest son was just grown to be a big lad, the father said to him one day, "Miska, my son, thou art now grown almost to manhood and we are so poor that I can feed thee no longer. The time has come when thou must go forth into the world and find employment. Go, son, and God will keep thee."

So Miska put a piece of bread in his knapsack, took his stout walking stick, kissed his mother, father and sisters and set forth into the world.

He wandered through seven times seven countries till all at once he met a very old, old man with a very long, long beard.

"God give thee good day, my grandfather," he said to the old man with reverence.

*Hungarian music is as colorful as this folk tale. It has curious runs, twists, and turns which Hungary owes to her gypsies. *Hungarian Rhapsodies* by **Liszt** and *Hungarian Dances* by **Brahms** have much national feeling.

"To thee, also, my son," said the man. "Where art thou going and what dost thou seek?"

"I am going out into the world to seek a job," said the lad.

"Then come and serve me," said the man, "for I am in need of a servant. True, I can't pay thee much but serve me for a year and I will give thee something."

Now Miska was glad to find work; so he went home with the old man, agreeing to accept for his services whatever the old man would pay. For a year he served his master obediently and faithfully and as he was a clever lad, industrious and honest, his master was well content; but when the year was up and Miska was dismissed, the old man gave him his blessing and nothing more for his labor except a little nut.

Very sad at heart, the lad started out toward home. His family were so poor. They needed so much in their hut and here for all a year's work he was bringing home nothing, nothing at all save a nut. He walked and he walked and he walked till at last he became so hungry that he decided to eat his nut.

"Such paltry pay as this means naught to my family," he said. And with that he cracked the nut. But look what happened then! Out of the nut there came running many tiny horses and many tiny cattle and many tiny sheep, and when they touched the ground, these animals grew and grew until they were the size of

ordinary horses, ordinary cattle and ordinary sheep. Miska's heart leapt for joy. What a treasure he had now! But in another moment those animals ran away, scattering over the plain. He could not keep them together and he saw they would all be lost. So he sat down on his fur coat and bowed his head for grief.

But all at once there appeared with a mighty clashing and clanking a very giant of a man whose head was made of iron. And the iron man said, "What ails thee?"

And Miska replied: "Good sir, how can I help but be sad when I worked a year for a nut and having no more sense than to crack that nut just now, I found all these animals here came springing out of the nut. And they are so many in number that I cannot drive them home."

"A hard task, truly," said the man. "But I have an offer to make thee. I will

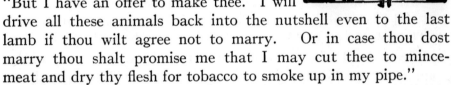

drive all these animals back into the nutshell even to the last lamb if thou wilt agree not to marry. Or in case thou dost marry thou shalt promise me that I may cut thee to mince-meat and dry thy flesh for tobacco to smoke up in my pipe."

Well, what could the poor lad do? He wasn't at that moment thinking much of the girls and he wanted beyond aught else to drive those flocks and herds back to his needy family. So he gave his word and agreed.

Then the Man-With-The-Iron-Head whistled three times very loudly and he lifted his great whip which was such an one as horse-herds use on the far-stretching plains of Hungary and he cracked it three times in the air. And lo! all those vast herds of horses, of vanishing cows and sheep came running from all directions. They began to grow smaller and smaller until each tiny animal was scarcely bigger than a pin-head. Then they crept back into the nutshell crowding over each other even to the last lamb. And when they were all inside, the nutshell closed again and there was the treasure safe. So Miska shouted for joy and he took the nut in his hand and continued on his way homeward.

Reaching the little hut where all his poor family lived, he cracked the nut on the doorstep and out there sprang in a moment all those beautiful animals. Well, the poor man and his wife and all their daughters cheered and they rounded the animals up and got some young herdsmen to tend them. They took Miska into the hut and made much of the lad and they listened while he told them all that happened in the year. Then they sold some of the animals and bought themselves fields and vineyards until they became in time the richest farmers in seven counties. And they took good care of the beasts, and they took good care of the farm. And all of them worked and prospered. But then it chanced one day that the farmer said to his son:

"Miska, the time has come for thee to raise a family of thine own and I have already selected a worthy lass for thee to marry."

Then the heart of Miska was sad for now he wished to marry. And he said: "Father, thou knowest that I cannot marry unless I am ready to die; for the iron-headed man will come and cut me up into mince-meat and dry my flesh for tobacco. Thou knowest I cannot marry." But the father only laughed.

"The iron-headed man was joking. Moreover, it is certain he does not live in these parts and will never hear of thy wedding. In case he should appear, which is really not at all probable, I will prepare a race horse ready with saddle and bridle, so thou canst leap on his back and gallop away in a twinkling."

Well, they laid their plans for a wedding with a mighty baking of cakes, with sewing on bridal garments and many grand preparations. But on the night of the feast when the guests were all very merry with dancing, eating and drinking, suddenly in the room a clashing sound was heard, a sound like the clanking of iron, and there appeared looming up above the heads of the guests the Man-With-The-Iron-Head, laughing with fiendish glee.

"Hey, boy," he said to Miska, "thou hast married just in time —in the nick of time for me. For this very day, my lad, I used my last bit of tobacco!"

But Miska leapt out through the window, straight on his horse's back. Like a whirlwind he rode away. The iron-headed man jumped after him. He ran at full speed at his heels.

Well, they raced and they raced and they raced through seven times seven countries and beyond the shining glass mountains till Miska outdistanced the iron man. Then he came to a little white cottage where lived a little old woman.

"God give thee good day, my grandmother," Miska said.

"To thee likewise," said the old woman. "But why didst thou come here, where not even a bird can come?"

"I'm running, granny," said Miska, "into the great world."

"My son," replied the old woman, "if thou art running away for some wrong-doing of thine own, then thou must turn back."

"I've done nothing wrong," said Miska. "I'm running from the iron man." So the woman invited him in and said she had a little dog who would bark if the iron-headed man came as near as seventy miles. And she cooked a very good dinner and Miska ate with relish till the dog began to bark. Then the woman hurried him off but she gave him before he went a kerchief of many colors, and a little twisted cake, both of which gifts she bade him keep with very great care as they would one day serve him well.

Then Miska thanked the old woman and once again raced forth through seven times seven countries and over other glass mountains till he came to another white cottage where lived another old woman. And he greeted her politely as he had greeted the other and the old woman asked him in and cooked him a very good meal and he stayed till her little dog barked, when this old woman, too, gave him a twisted cake and a kerchief of many colors and hurried him off on his way. And he raced as swift as the wind through seven times seven countries and over other glass mountains till he came to another house where lived another old woman. And he greeted her politely and the old woman asked him in and he stayed till her little dog barked when this old woman, too, gave him a cake and a kerchief and hurried him off on his way. But before he went she said:

"For seven days ride toward the sunset. With the next day's dawn thou wilt see a wall of endless fire. Beat that fire with thy kerchiefs, and a passage will open for thee. Then as thou ridest through, cast the three twisted cakes backward over thy head and see what will come to pass."

So Miska thanked the old woman and rode away like the wind. And by and by he saw before him a mighty sheet of fire, rising straight up to the sky. He beat the flames three times with the kerchiefs that had been given him; a passage opened at once and he rode in safety through, though there towered on either side of him great flaming walls of fire. And as he rode he cast the three cakes backward over his head. Lo, they became in a moment three enormous dogs. And the first dog yelped, "My name's Goodear! I can hear a blade of grass growing at a distance of seventy miles!" And the second dog yelped, "My name's Ironstrong, for I am as strong as iron!" And the third dog yelped, "My name's Weigh-much! I can press hard rock into dust merely by force of my weight!" And the dogs ran along after Miska.

THE MAGIC GARDEN

But now as he passed through the flames, the iron-headed man came raging straight to the edge of the fire. The passage closed in a twinkling before his very nose. Then the iron man shouted with wrath, "Do not rejoice, thou rascal! One of these days I'll catch thee and thou shalt end as smoke and ashes in my pipe!"

And he settled down to wait before the wall of flames till a passage should open for him.

But Miska now found himself in a very beautiful land, lovely and green as a garden and embroidered with bright-colored flowers. In time he came to a cottage where he found an old woman spinning before her spinning wheel and with her a beautiful girl who was combing her golden hair.

"Whither goest thou?" asked the old woman.

"To get a good job," said the boy.

"Then stay and serve me," said the woman.

So Miska stayed with the woman and served her in all things well. He ploughed and he harvested for her and he went hunting with his three dogs. But now the beautiful maiden with the hair of fine spun gold came to love Miska dearly and Miska loved the maiden; for the bride he had left at home had been of his father's choosing and not of his own selection. So these two beautiful young folk loved each other well. But the maiden felt in her heart one dark little seed of doubt that the story Miska had told of opening a passage of entrance through the wall of Endless Fire by beating it thrice with three kerchiefs was not really true. And the dark little seed of doubt kept growing and growing and growing till all her soul was dark. And she resolved in secret to test the magic qualities of the kerchiefs of many colors. So one day while the boy was working far off in a field, she went to the Endless Fire and she beat it thrice with the kerchiefs. Then lo, the passage opened, and the terrible iron-headed man who had been lying in wait these days and days and days, came rushing through

17

at full speed, raging and
clashing and clanking. Seeing so dreadful a figure, the
maiden ran off in fear.

And now who comes
home but Miska, bringing his
three dogs with him and
suspecting nothing at all.
Watching him come, the iron
man hid behind a tree. There
he waited to catch the boy
without his protecting dogs.
Well, Miska came whistling
along, locked his dogs in the stable, and went to look for the girl.

Then out sprang the iron-headed man, clashing and clanking
and raging. In a twinkling Miska beheld him and made for the
nearest tree, climbing in no time at all up to its highest branches.
But the iron-headed man below laughed in an ugly way and cried,
"Thou cunning pup! Now I've caught thee, I have!"

Miska bethought him quickly what to do in this case. Quietly
he whispered the names of his three dogs, keeping his voice so
low that the man beneath did not hear him. But Goodear heard
him at once and said to the other dogs, "Our master is in danger."

So Ironstrong rose in his strength and kicked the stable to bits
and out flew the dogs in a hurry. Weigh-much jumped on the
iron man and pressed him out flat as a disk. Ironstrong picked
him up and tossed him so high in the air, that he did not fall back
for a week and then he was only dust!

Well, that was the end of the iron man but now what was
Miska to do? He felt that he must return to the family and
bride he had left and yet how he loved the maiden with the hair
of fine-spun gold. His heart was heavy within him and her heart

was heavy too. And much she reproached herself for doubting her young lover and letting the iron man in. But what could the poor things do? She gave the boy a ring and wept and wished him Godspeed. And Miska was soon on his way back to his family and bride. As he left the Endless Fire the three trusty dogs turned again into three twisted cakes. Miska picked them up and returned them to the old women together with the kerchiefs and he thanked them all for their help.

Thus he came again to the farm. His parents and his sisters all received him with joy, but his heart was heavy within him for loss of the beautiful girl. Yet when he asked for the lass his father had chosen as bride, his parents hung their heads.

"We all thought thee dead," they said. "And thy bride has married a lad who lives in a neighboring village. They are very happy together." Well, that was no bad news for Miska; he might very well have rejoiced, but still he could feel only sadness; for

how now could he get back through the wall of Endless Fire to the lovely golden-haired maiden? As he thought of her with longing he twisted the ring on his finger, wishing with all his heart that he could see her at once. And lo, there she stood before him; for that was a magic ring she had given him at parting. Blushing and smiling for joy, the golden-haired maid stood before him. And they were married next day and the other bride danced at the wedding and they all lived happily ever after.

The Youth Who Wanted Some Fun
A Welsh Fairy Tale

FAR UP among the mountains in Wales there lies a little hollow called The Elves' Dell, where a young man named Tudur ap Einion used to pasture his master's sheep. One summer night Tudur was returning to the lowlands with his flock when he began to loiter along and grumble to himself.

"Tending sheep!" he grumbled. "Such stupid business this is! Would a gay lad like me might have a little fun!"

Then suddenly he saw, perched near him on a stone, a little man in moss breeches with a fiddle under his arm. His coat was made of birch leaves, he wore a gorse flower for a cap and his feet were shod with beetles' wings.

Tudur naturally loved music and dancing; for, in Wales, every village has its annual music festival. The *crwth*, a stringed instrument played with a bow, is typically Welsh. *Men of Harlech* is the national anthem of Wales.

THE MAGIC GARDEN

As Tudur stared open-mouthed at the little man, the latter took up his fiddle, which was nothing more than a stringed wooden spoon, and ran his fingers across it.

"*Nos dawch! Nos dawch!*" said the little man, which means in English, "Good-evening to you! Good-evening to you!"

"*Ac i chwithan!*" replied Tudur, which is, being interpreted, "The same to you!"

"You are fond of dancing, Tudur!" went on the little man. "Why do anything so stupid as to tend sheep? Tarry here awhile, and you shall see some of the best dancers in Wales. I—," he swelled out his chest as he spoke, "I am their musician."

"But if you are a musician, where is your harp?" asked Tudur, loitering still more slowly. "No Welshman can dance unless someone plays on the harp."

"Harp!" cried the little man scornfully. "I can make people dance with my fiddle better than any harper!" Then he leered with a smile so ugly that Tudur shivered for a moment. But he was very curious about that spoon. So he asked:

"Is that a fiddle, that stringed wooden spoon you have in your hand?"

For answer the little man nodded and started to play.

At that Tudur saw hundreds of pretty little sprites come tripping out through the dusk, some dressed in white, some in blue and some bearing glowworms for torches. So lightly did they step that not a blade of grass nor any flower was crushed beneath their weight and they all made curtsies to Tudur. Then Tudur forgot that creepy feeling the little man had given him. Doffing his cap, he bowed politely to each of the little sprites.

21

Presently the little minstrel drew his bow across the strings of his instrument, and the music he produced seemed to Tudur so enchanting, that he turned farther and farther away from his sheep and listened, open-mouthed.

At sound of the sweet melody, the fairies (if fairies they were) ranged themselves in groups and began to dance. Round and round they went as the bow of the little minstrel flew. All the dancing Tudur had ever seen could not compare with this. His feet began to keep time to the music. He longed to step into the magic circle. Yet there was something in his breast that warned him away from it, and he heard his sheep calling him to his duties down the mountain.

"Come, Tudur, join in the dance and make merry!" the little man cried.

Tudur's feet beat a faster tattoo, yet he still gave ear to the call of his sheep.

"Nay, nay," he said, "dance on, dance my little beauties! Dance on! I take my sheep down the mountain."

Neverthless he did not go, he did not even turn away. He lingered and yielded himself more and more to the entertainment before him. The music became faster and the dance grew wilder and wilder.

"Come, Tudur, join in the dance and make merry!" the little man cried again. Tudur began to sway with his whole body in time to the rhythm. He swayed and he swayed while the bleating of his sheep sounded more and more faintly in the distance.

"Come, Tudur, join in the dance and make merry!" the little man cried a third time, with a sweep of his bow across the strings that seemed to the shepherd sweeter than anything he had ever heard in all his life before.

Then Tudur flung all thought of his sheep to the winds. With a bound he threw hinself into the midst of the circle. Hurling his cap in the air, he cried, "Now for it! Play away, fiddler! Play away!" And he gave him- self wholly up to the dance.

But what a change! No sooner was he within the ring that had seemed so pleasant when he stood looking on from without, than in a twinkling, all was altered. The gorse-blossom cap vanished from the minstrel's head, a pair of goat's horns branched out instead, and his face became as black as soot. The creatures that a moment before he had thought so beautiful, now became ugly goats and dogs, while some took the shape of foxes and cats. And in the midst of these Tudur went dancing on! At length the motion grew so furious that Tudur could not make out the forms of the dancers at all. They whirled round and round him so rapidly that they looked like a wheel of fire. And still he flung himself about and waved his arms in time to their music. How gladly he would have torn himself away, but it seemed to him that he could not. In the midst of the ugly company he had chosen, he was forced to dance on and on and on.

THE MAGIC GARDEN

Next morning, Tudur's master went up the mountain to see what had become of his sheep and his shepherd. He found the flock safe and sound halfway down to the valley, but was astonished to see Tudur spinning around like mad in the midst of the hollow, all by himself.

"What in the world is the silly lad doing?" he cried.

"O Master, Master, stop me!" shouted Tudur.

"Stop yourself!" replied the master. "In the name of Heaven, stop yourself! Stop yourself!"

At these words Tudur suddenly stopped and blinked his eyes. There was no ugly circle about him. There was only the morning sunlight, the rocky crags above, and the sheep awaiting his tendance on the green flower-sprinkled mountain pastures.

"Tudur ap Einion, let me not find you deserting your sheep again!" cried his master.

Tudur hung his head and went foolishly back to his charges.

The Trial by Fire
A MAORI FOLK TALE FROM NEW ZEALAND*

IN OLD days there lived in New Zealand beneath the towering mountains beside a bright blue lake, a lovely, graceful brown maiden. She moved gloriously in the sunlight, clad in her bright-colored garments, against the patterned background of enormous giant ferns and the snow of great white blossoms. Her name was Hine Moa; she was daughter of a Maori Chieftain, and many were the youths who sought her for a wife. At length there came to her father, asking her hand in marriage, a fine strong Prince, son of a neighboring Chieftain who lived across the lake. No sooner had Hine Moa seen this magnificent fellow than she lost her heart and wished to be his bride. Her father also looked with eyes of favor on the young Prince. He received him with ceremony, with dancing and much feasting.

But there was in this Maori tribe a jealous youth, named Tai. Tai loved the Princess madly. He must show her he was stronger

*The wealth of color among Maoris and other South Sea peoples inspired the modern French painter, Paul Gauguin, who lived among them, to paint more gorgeous colors than any artist since Fra Angelico and the early Italians.

THE MAGIC GARDEN

than his rival! So he challenged the Prince to meet him in a public wrestling match where the Princess would be looking on. But soon the great day came with the Princess and her father among the spectators at the event. Long and hard the two youths wrestled but at last the Prince threw Tai, pinned his shoulders to the ground and held him down before the very eyes of the Princess.

Then Tai crept off in a fury to think up trickery and deceit. Now to Maoris their Chief was sacred. To steal his food was like stealing from the gods. So Tai, sneaking by night to the Chieftain's storehouse, crept past the guardian figure of the god beside it and stole some sweet potatoes. And when the theft was discovered he accused the Prince of the crime. Then the joyous feasting ended. Anger was in men's hearts. And the Chief condemned the Prince to a punishment so terrible it took all his courage to face it. He must pass through the Valley of Fire, through all the unspeakable horrors of a great volcanic cave! If guilty, the Chief declared, he would die in the flames. If innocent, he would pass through safely.

The Maoris, native inhabitants of New Zealand, are the most intelligent, cultured, and gifted primitive people in the world. They have a wealth of folk tales and a keen sense of beauty as their wood-carving shows.

So the Chieftain's warriors took the unfortunate young Prince and led him out through a wild, uncanny land of dark desolation beneath a frowning volcano that grimly brooded on the moment when it should erupt with fire. White puffs of steam burst continually here, there, and everywhere out of the rocky hillsides; hot lakes—pink, blue and yellow—gleamed slimily at the base of brilliantly colored terraces, formed by the hot, flowing water. And with a terrific blast, a geyser shot up hissing amid a  white burst of steam to fall back in scalding water over all the ground around. Crossing this seething inferno, the tribesmen thrust the young Prince into the terrible cave. Leaving the light of day, he plunged into hideous darkness. About him leaped sulphurous flames, terrific against the blackness. He was scarcely able to breathe; the fumes of the fire were stifling; and, at every step he took, the earth beneath his feet quivered and throbbed and trembled. It rumbled unearthly mutterings, threatening some furious convulsion. He passed by ugly pools of foul, black, seething mud, fiendishly bubbling and boiling. He crawled over steaming rocks, past streams of molten lava that flowed in sinister fashion, creeping over the ground like some great sullen snake. One misstep and he would be lost! He would be sunk in some hideous pool!

28

THE MAGIC GARDEN

But the heart of the Prince was innocent. He had been guilty of no crime, so he passed in safety out of the cave and returned to his father's tribe on the other side of the lake.

But now what a sadness was on him! He had lost his beautiful maiden. In the home of his father, he grieved. Nothing could comfort him. Months passed; and, at last, unable to bear any longer the sorrow of separation, the Prince called to him a messenger whom he could safely trust. "Seek Hine Moa," he said, "and deliver this message from my heart."

So the messenger went in secret to the village across the lake. In secret he found Hine Moa and told her the heart of her lover was forever crying for her. Hine Moa was deeply moved.

"Tell my beloved that I will come to him," she said. "On the night of the next full moon I will come!"

But the villainous Tai, ever skulking about and spying upon the Princess, overheard the words she had spoken and hurried off to her father to tell him what had occurred.

The night of the full moon came. Gloriously it shone in a glitter of silver over the lake. Hine Moa stole from her home and down to the edge of the water. She expected to find a canoe there to take her across the lake. But, lo, when she arrived every one of the many canoes drawn up on the shore of the lake, was guarded by a powerful warrior. Her father knew of her plans! Some one had betrayed her! The girl did not hesitate. She plunged at once into the water. Putting forth all her strength, borne up by her love and longing, she swam with tremendous effort all the long distance across the moonlit stretch of rippling waves. When dawn rose red on the world, she dragged herself exhausted up on the opposite shore. Her lover found her there and great was the joy of the two at being again united. But their happiness, alas, was not of long duration. It ended all too soon.

Almost at once they saw on the lake a bevy of war canoes, each manned by thirty men and sent by Hine Moa's father. Warriors sprang out on shore and danced a hideous war dance. Step by step they advanced, grimacing with eyes and tongues till they looked like grotesque savage masks. Ever more frenzied they grew in the steps of that terrible dance. In a short time, maddened by the dancing, they would spring on the warriors the Prince now gathered together. Spears would clash! Blood would flow! The battle would be on!

However, there was one person, a woman, who knew that Tai had stolen the sacred food. Heretofore, fear of Tai had kept her from telling what she knew. But now with all the warriors of her tribe about to face death because of Tai's lies, she ran to the Chief and told him the truth.

Then the old Chief, crossing the lake, suddenly appeared in all his dignity before his dance-crazed warriors. Stilling their tumult, he called for the Prince's father. And the two Chiefs, standing beside the lake, greeted each other in friendly fashion by touching foreheads and noses in the ancient Maori manner. Then the Prince brought Hine Moa forward. And while Tai stood by, angry and thwarted, Hine Moa's father declared that she should wed the Prince. Thus the two were married and were happy together at last.

East O' the Sun and West O' the Moon
A Norse Folk Tale

Once on a time there lived a poor husbandman who had so many children that none had food or clothing enough. Pretty children they were, but the prettiest was the youngest daughter, who was so very lovely that there was no end to her loveliness.

'Twas on a Thursday evening late in the fall of the year. The weather was wild outside; rain fell and the wind blew till the walls of the cottage shook. There they all sat around the fire, busy with this thing and that. But all at once, something gave three taps on the window-pane,—tap! tap! tap! The father went out to see what it was, and, when he got out of doors, what should he see but a big, White Bear.

"Good evening to you," said the Bear.

"The same to you," said the man.

"Will you give me your youngest daughter?" said the Bear. "If you will, I'll make you as rich as you are poor tonight."

Well, the man would be glad to be rich, but give up his daughter, no, that he wouldn't, he said. But the White Bear said, "Think it over; next Thursday night I'll come back and then you can give me your answer."

So the father went into the house and told them all that had happened. Now when the lassie heard how she could lighten the poverty of her parents and brothers and sisters, she said at once she would go. Let her family beg never so hard, go she would, she said. I can't say her packing gave her much trouble. She washed and mended her rags and made herself ready to start.

Next Thursday evening the White Bear came. She got on his back with her bundle and off they went through the woods.

"Are you afraid?" said the Bear.

"No, not at all," said the lassie.

So she rode a long, long way till they came to a great steep hill. The White Bear knocked on the face of the hill, a little door opened and they entered a castle, with rooms all lit up and gleaming, splendid with silver and gold. There, too, was a table laid. It was all as grand as could be. Then the White Bear gave the lassie a bell and told her to ring when she wanted anything.

Well, after she had eaten, she thought she would go to bed, and scarcely had she lifted the bell when she found herself in a room with a bed as fair and white as any one could wish to sleep in. But when she had put out her light she heard someone enter the room next hers, and there someone stayed until dawn. Night after night the same thing occurred. Not a single human being did the lassie see through the day but when all the lights were out, someone would enter the room next hers and sleep there

until the dawn. But always before the daylight appeared whoever it was, was up and off, so as never to be seen.

Things went on well for a while, but all day long the lassie
had not a soul to talk to except for the White Bear and she knew
not whether it was man or beast who slept in the next room at
night. So at last she grew silent and sorrowful. Then the White
Bear came and said, "What troubles you, my lassie? Here you
have everything heart can wish. You have only to ring the bell
and whatever you want is brought you."

"Nay then," said the lassie, "I am lonely. Who is it that
sleeps in the room next mine?" At that the Bear begged her to
ask no such questions. "Trust me," he said. "Don't try to find
out and in due time you will know." Now the lassie was grateful to the Bear and fond of him, but in spite of what he said, she
grew more and more sorrowful and more and more lonely. Who
was it that shared the castle with her? Who was it? Who was
it? Who was it? She was forever thinking of that one thing alone.
All day long and all night long she wondered and fretted. Still
for a long, long time she obeyed the Bear and did not try to find
out. But at last she could stand it no longer. In the dead of
night she got up, lit a candle and slipped softly into the next
room. There asleep on a bed she saw the loveliest Prince one
ever set eyes on. Slowly she crept up to him, bent over and
kissed him. But as she did so, three drops of hot tallow fell
from her candle onto his shirt and awoke him.

"Alas! What have you done?" he cried. "Now you have
spoiled all that was gained by the months you were faithful to
me. Had you held out only this one year, you would have set me
free. For a witch has cast a spell upon me, so that I am a white
bear by day and a man only at night. A year of good faith and
you would have saved me, but now all is over between us. Back
I must go to the castle *East o' the Sun and West o' the Moon.*

There I must marry the witch with a nose three ells long. She must now be the wife for me."

The lassie wept but there was no help for it. Go he must, he said. Then she asked if she mightn't go with him.

No, she mightn't, he said.

"Tell me the way there, then," said she, "and I'll search you out over all the world, no matter how hard is the journey."

"But there is no way to that place," cried the Prince. "It lies *East o' the Sun and West o' the Moon*, that is all I can tell you."

Next morning when the lassie awoke, both Prince and castle were gone. There she lay on a little green patch in the midst of the gloomy, thick wood, and by her side lay the same bundle of rags which she had brought with her from home.

When she had rubbed the sleep out of her eyes and wept at her loss of the Prince, she set out on her journey and walked for many days, until she came to a lofty crag under which an old woman sat tossing a golden apple. Her the lassie asked if she knew the way to the castle that lay *East o' the Sun and West o' the Moon*. But the old woman answered:

"All I know about it is that it lies *East o' the Sun and West o' the Moon* and thither you'll come late or never. But go on to my next neighbor. Maybe she will be able to tell you more." Then she gave the lassie her golden apple. "It might prove useful," she said.

So the lassie went on a long, long time till she came to another crag, under which sat another old woman with a golden carding-comb. Her the lassie asked if she knew the way to the castle that lay *East o' the Sun and West o' the Moon*, but this old woman likewise knew nothing about the matter.

"Go on to my next neighbor," she said. "Maybe she can tell you." And she gave the lassie the carding-comb and bade her take it with her.

So the lassie went on and on, a far, far way and a weary,

weary time till at last she came
to another crag under which sat
another old woman spinning with
a golden spinning wheel. Her too
she asked if she knew the way to
the castle that lay *East o' the Sun
and West o' the Moon*. It was the
same thing over again. She knew
nothing, but this old woman said:

"Go to the East Wind and
ask him. Maybe he knows those
parts and can blow you thither."
Then she gave the lassie her
golden spinning wheel, and bade
her take it with her.

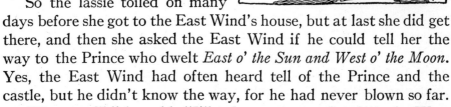

So the lassie toiled on many
days before she got to the East Wind's house, but at last she did get
there, and then she asked the East Wind if he could tell her the
way to the Prince who dwelt *East o' the Sun and West o' the Moon*.
Yes, the East Wind had often heard tell of the Prince and the
castle, but he didn't know the way, for he had never blown so far.

"If you will," he said, "I'll take you to my brother, the West
Wind. Maybe he knows, for he's much stronger than I. Just
get up on my back and I'll carry you thither."

Yes, she got on his back, and I should just think they went
briskly along till they came to the West Wind's house. Then
the lassie asked the West Wind if he knew how to get to the
castle *East o' the Sun and West o' the Moon*.

"Nay," said the West Wind, "so far I've never blown, but if
you'll get on my back, I'll carry you to our brother the South Wind.
He has flapped his wings far and wide. Maybe he can tell you."

So she got on his back and travelled to the South Wind,
and wasn't long on the way. And the lassie asked the South Wind

if he knew the way to the castle *East o' the Sun and West o' the Moon.*

"Well, I've blustered about in most places in my time," answered the South Wind, "but so far I've never blown. Just get up on my back, and I'll carry you to my brother, the North Wind. He is the strongest of all of us, and if he doesn't know where it is, you'll never find anyone to tell you."

So she got on his back, and away he went.

When they got to the North Wind's house, he was so wild and cross that they felt his cold icy puffs when they were a long way off. "What do you want?" he roared in a voice that made them shiver. Then the lassie asked the North Wind if he knew the way to the castle *East o' the Sun and West o' the Moon.*

"Yes!" roared the North Wind. "I know well enough! Once in my life I blew an aspen leaf thither, but I was so tired I couldn't blow a puff for ever so many days after. If you really wish to go so far and aren't afraid to come along, I'll take you on my back and see if I can blow you thither."

Yes, with all her heart! She must and would get there if she could possibly do it. And as for fear, no matter how madly he went, she wouldn't be afraid at all.

Early next morning they started. The North Wind puffed himself up, and made himself so stout, 'twas gruesome to look upon him. Off they went through the air, as if they would never stop till they got to the end of the world. Down below a storm raged.

They tore on and on—no one can believe how far they went— and all the time they still went over the sea. The North Wind got more and more weary, and so out of breath he could scarcely puff; his wings drooped and drooped, till he sunk so low that the crests of the waves went dashing over his heels.

"Are you afraid?" asked the North Wind.

No, she wasn't afraid.

But they weren't very far from the land, and the North Wind still had strength enough to throw her up on the shore. Now at last she was under the windows of the castle which lay *East o' the Sun and West o' the Moon.*

All through the day the lassie saw no one, but toward night she began to play with her golden apple, tossing it into the air. At that, out came Long-nose, who was going to marry the Prince.

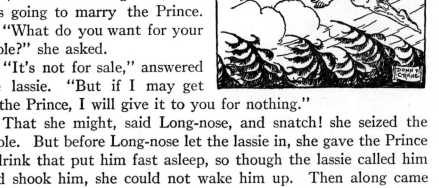

"What do you want for your apple?" she asked.

"It's not for sale," answered the lassie. "But if I may get to the Prince, I will give it to you for nothing."

. That she might, said Long-nose, and snatch! she seized the apple. But before Long-nose let the lassie in, she gave the Prince a drink that put him fast asleep, so though the lassie called him and shook him, she could not wake him up. Then along came Long-nose and drove her out again.

Next day the same thing happened. So long as it was light the gloomy old castle was still as death and no one even looked out of it. But at nightfall signs of life awoke, and when the lassie began to card with the golden carding-comb, out came Long-nose to buy it.

"It's not for sale for gold or money," answered the lassie. "But if I may get to the Prince, you shall have it." Now when the lassie went up this time she found the Prince fast asleep as before, and all she called, and all she shook, she couldn't wake him up. Then along came Long-nose and chased her out again.

So the next night the lassie sat down under the castle window and began to spin with her golden spinning wheel. Long-nose must have the spinning wheel too; so in went the lassie once more. But this time, the Prince's servants had told him how a beautiful lassie had come and wept over him and called him two nights running. So, when Long-nose gave him his night drink, he poured it out secretly on the floor, and the lassie found, to her joy, that his eyes were wide open. Then she told him the whole long story of how she had made the far, far journey and the Prince wept and smiled and had great joy of her coming.

"You've got here just in the nick of time," cried he, "for to-morrow's to be my wedding. Be waiting at the gate and you'll see what you will see."

Well, the wedding was to be the next night in the dark, for witches and trolls can never endure the daylight. But when the time came, the Prince announced:

"Ere I marry, I'll see what my bride can do. Here is my wedding shirt, but on it are three spots of tallow. I'll have no other for a bride save her who can wash it clean."

"No great thing to do," said Long-nose. So when the moon stood high, shining over the tree tops, she hung a caldron of boiling lye in a clearing in the woods. Thither came running, tumbling, scolding, a whole pack of trolls and witches, long-nosed, red-eyed, ugly, a hideous sight to see. First Long-nose began to wash. She washed as hard as she could, but the more she rubbed and scrubbed the bigger grew the spots. "Oh, you can't wash! Let me try!" another troll woman cried, and wash, wash, wash,—every one in turn scrubbed away on that shirt. But the more they washed, the blacker and uglier grew the shirt, till at last it was black all over as if it had been up the chimney.

"Ah!" cried the Prince, "you're none of you worth a straw.

THE MAGIC GARDEN

I'll have none of you for my bride. Why! look, outside the gate
there sits a beggar lass. I'll be bound she knows how to wash
better than your whole pack. Come in, lassie!" he shouted.

So in came the lassie, and almost before she had taken the
shirt and dipped it in the water, it was white as the driven snow.

"You are the lassie for me!" cried the Prince. Then the
witches and trolls rushed raging upon him, but ah! while they
had been washing, the night had slowly waned. Just then the
sun came up. The moment it pierced the mist and gloom and
shone directly on Long-nose, she burst, like an empty bubble.
The whole pack of trolls uttered horrid shrieks and hurried away
toward the castle, but it was no use at all. The instant the sun
struck them squarely, they every one of them vanished.

As for the Prince and Princess, they took hold of hands and
flitted away as far as they could from the castle that lay *East o'
the Sun and West o' the Moon.*

The Maiden, the Knight, and the Waterfall

A Roumanian Fairy Tale

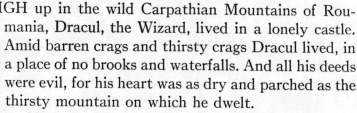

HIGH up in the wild Carpathian Mountains of Roumania, Dracul, the Wizard, lived in a lonely castle. Amid barren crags and thirsty crags Dracul lived, in a place of no brooks and waterfalls. And all his deeds were evil, for his heart was as dry and parched as the thirsty mountain on which he dwelt.

Now there also lived in Roumania in those days a fine young Knight, a Boyar, who was trying to learn the secret that would destroy the Wizard's evil spells. And Dracul, fearing lest he should succeed, followed him by stealth until he got him alone by night. Then in the darkness of a wood he spoke magic words and turned the Knight into a sword. Laughing with fiendish glee, he stuck that sword in a scabbard by his side. But as the days went by Dracul ceased to laugh. For he could not manage that sword. When he meant to destroy good men and women, the sword would leap from his scabbard and defend them, defeating the Wizard in every plan he made.

Well, the fame of this strange sword at last reached the ears of old Michael, a great lord and hospodar of Roumania. So having need of such a magnificent weapon to administer justice on his own estates, he set out for Dracul's castle to ask the Wizard to lend him the sword. And Michael took with him on that journey his beautiful daughter who had the loveliest hair in the world. Sitting erect on her horse, the maiden waited for her father outside Dracul's castle while Michael went in to make his request.

Being thoroughly sick of a sword he couldn't manage, Dracul was about to hand it over gladly and without reservations to Michael when his eyes chanced to light on the beautiful hair of the old man's daughter, whom he could see through the window.

40

THE MAGIC GARDEN

Then to Dracul, who dwelt on that dry and thirsty mountain, it seemed that the maiden's glorious hair looked like a waterfall, a shining stream leaping down a hillside. So he said to the father:

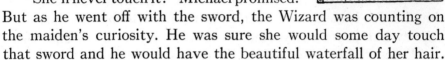

"I'll lend you my sword. But your daughter must never touch it. If she does I'll seize all her hair!"

"She'll never touch it!" Michael promised. But as he went off with the sword, the Wizard was counting on the maiden's curiosity. He was sure she would some day touch that sword and he would have the beautiful waterfall of her hair.

After that all went well for a time. Michael told his daughter she must never touch the sword. And she never did. Meantime, the sword performed wonders for Michael, always leaping out of the scabbard to protect the innocent and oppressed. But one day Michael went off hunting with bow and arrows, leaving the sword at home. Then his daughter, who was quietly weaving, heard a voice cry out from the sword:

"O maiden, save me! I'm a Knight, a Boyar, imprisoned by the Wizard in this sword! Touch me, O maiden! Touch me once only and I shall be free!"

Then the maiden was deeply moved. She thought only of the imprisoned Knight. So she rose and touched the sword. At once it was shattered. From its flashing pieces sprang a fine young Boyar in armor of steel. Kneeling, he kissed the hem of her gown and said: "O lovely one, I thank thee!"

Then seeing her so beautiful, he was loath to leave her. But he felt called to do great deeds in the world. So he said at last:

"Now that thou hast freed me, I shall go forth and seek! Seek until I find! Farewell, sweet maiden! I go to learn how Dracul's evil power can be destroyed!"

And with one last look at the maiden, he was off. But scarcely had he gone when serving women rushed in, crying out that Michael's huntsmen had returned without him. For he had disappeared when they were almost home. Then the maiden knew Dracul had seized her father because she had touched the sword and freed the Knight imprisoned in it. And now she had neither Knight nor father! But she set out alone to face the Wizard up among those wild mountains. However, she was still in the land of meadows when she came on Dracul himself. Kneeling before him, she pleaded with him to set her father free. But he only seized her hair savagely, covetously. And he cried in a parched, cracked voice:

"Before I free your father, I'll have your hair!"

Now at this time there lived on that same mountain with the Wizard an old, old man, the true spirit of the mountain. And this Old Man of the Mountain, long concerned because those heights were so dry and waterless, had cried to the Fairy who dwelt in the flowery green meadows below. "O Fairy of the Meadows, you have brooks and streams! I beg you, I pray you, to find me a waterfall that will leap with laughter down these dry barren slopes and make them burst into bloom!"

Then the Fairy was sorry for the Old Man of the Mountain. So she started out into the world to find him a waterfall. She was riding a horse but soon she made herself as small as a bumble bee and turned her steed into a butterfly. Then she sat down beneath the grass to consider what she should do. Thus, all unseen, she was close to the maiden when the Wizard demanded her hair.

At once the Fairy was filled with pity for the maiden. All unnoticed by the Wizard, she leapt on her butterfly, flew close to the maiden's ear and whispered, "Courage! Don't give Dracul your hair! I'm a Fairy! I'll help you!"

At that the maiden sprang to her feet and her locks, slipping like water through the Wizard's fingers, rippled out of his reach.

THE MAGIC GARDEN

"Begone!" she cried. "I'll keep my hair and still set my father free! Begone! Begone from my sight!"

Then the Wizard, snarling, vanished in a mist. And when the Fairy had made herself big again the maiden told her all that had happened to her father, the Knight and herself.

"We'll still save your father!" the Fairy said. And changing her butterfly into a horse again, she bade the maiden to mount behind her and together they galloped away up the mountain side toward the Wizard's castle. And as they rode the Fairy noticed how the maiden's beautiful hair sparkled in the sunlight. And if the wind blew a single thread to the ground, it turned into a strand of glistening dew drops. Then the Fairy thought:

"If one thread of her hair makes a strand of dew drops, surely all of it would make a waterfall!" And she guessed why the Wizard, he who dwelt amid barren crags and thirsty crags, was so determined to have that hair. But though she herself wanted a waterfall for the Old Man of the Mountain, she would not steal one.

43

Riding in friendly fashion together, the maiden and the Fairy were nearing the Wizard's castle when suddenly the Knight of the Sword came dashing up and drew rein before them. Fine in his armor he looked and his face bore a look of triumph as of one who has succeeded in some difficult task.

"Greetings, most lovely maiden!" he cried. "I have it! I've found the secret which will destroy Dracul's evil power!"

Then the maiden smiled her joy at what he had accomplished. And she told him all that had befallen her and how, but for the Fairy, Dracul would have seized her hair. At that the Knight was sore distressed. Deeply he grieved to think he had left her to meet such danger alone and to think she had suffered so much because she had set him free. And he cried:

"I will not leave thee again until we have rendered Dracul powerless!" Then he sprang from his horse. "I shall tell this good Fairy the secret I've learned! To her I yield the honor of destroying the Wizard's power. For I shall stay with thee, maiden! I shall stay here and keep thee safe!"

And with that he whispered the secret to the Fairy. Then as the maiden looked up with utter confidence into his face, he lifted her down from the Fairy's horse and set her up on his own fine steed, while the Fairy, mightily pleased with her mission, rode on alone to Dracul's castle. At the gate she blew three blasts on a silver horn that hung there and in answer to her summons Dracul himself appeared.

"I'm weary, sir!" she said. "I crave a room to rest in. But above all, I crave a goblet of cool, fresh water."

Now Dracul had no water to give, as the Fairy knew full well. But he dared not offend so powerful a Fairy, so he showed her to a splendid chamber and went off, saying he would fetch her a drink. Then he hurried to the deep, dark dungeon where he kept Michael, the hospodar.

THE MAGIC GARDEN

"Aha, hospodar!" he mocked. "Thou who rulest over rats in a dungeon! I have stolen thy lovely daughter and taken her off to a far distant land. Never shalt thou see her more!"

The words were false, but the Wizard knew that they would bring tears to Michael's eyes. And while the poor father wept, Dracul caught the tears in a golden goblet. Then he carried them off to the Fairy and said, "Here is your cool, fresh water!"

But from what the Knight had told her, the Fairy knew what would be in the goblet and just what she must do. So when the Wizard had left her, she waved her wand and at once a beautiful maiden sprang up from those tears.

"Dear child!" the Fairy said. "You are all goodness, tenderness and beauty, for you were born of loving tears. When the Wizard sees you, the evil will die in his heart."

"Aye!" the Tear-Maiden answered gently. "Whoever looks deep into my eyes is melted at once with compassion."

Soon back came Dracul, blustering, into the Fairy's chamber. But there he saw, beautiful before him, her eyes beaming with sorrowful gentleness and tenderness, the Tear-Maiden.

"Whence came you?" he cried in a fright and clapped his hands over his eyes. "Away! Away! Away!" But the Tear-Maiden only continued to beam on him gently, softly, sorrowfully. And Dracul felt the light of her gaze go deep down into his heart. Slowly he dropped his fingers from his face and looked long and full into her eyes. Then his head fell on his breast, his shoulders drooped, his chest heaved and he burst into tears of repentance.

"This maiden will stay with you always," the Fairy said. "But only on condition that you bring me Michael, the hospodar, free!"

Without a word, Dracul turned away and hurried off to fetch Michael. Then the Fairy, running to the window, waved her kerchief to the Knight and the maiden. And the Knight, leaping up behind the maiden on the horse, came dashing on to the castle.

When the two entered the Fairy's chamber, there stood Michael free at last. And the maiden threw herself joyously into her father's arms while Dracul stood humbly by, once again looking deeply into the Tear-Maiden's eyes. And the Fairy said to the Knight:

"He will work no more wickedness. 'Twas a great deed you did when you discovered how to destroy his power to do evil!"

Then Michael's daughter knelt in gratitude before the Fairy.

"O you, who have brought us such joy!" she cried. "What can I do for you? My dearest possession I'd gladly give you!"

"Then if it should please you, but only if it should please you, I pray you to give me your hair," the Fairy said.

So the maiden gladly gave the Fairy the locks that all the power of the Wizard could not get from her. And the Knight said to the maiden:

"My fair one, thy beautiful hair will grow again, long and rippling as before! Meantime, thou art to me ever lovely. If thou wilt but say the word, I'd have thee for my wife!"

THE MAGIC GARDEN

And the maiden said the word. Then everyone was very happy and the Fairy took the maiden's hair back to the Old Man of the Mountain. From the highest crag on the mountain she hung that gleaming strand. Then suddenly, lo! it began to ripple and wave, and in another moment, down it gushed in a torrent, leaping from rock to rock, laughing, roaring, tumbling, flinging forth sheets of shining spray. And wherever it went, there the mountain burst into splendid bloom.

THE CATARACT OF LODORE

How does the water come down at Lodore?

* * *

Advancing and prancing and glancing
    and dancing,
Recoiling, turmoiling, and toiling,
    and boiling,
And gleaming and streaming and steaming
    and beaming,
And rushing and flushing and brushing
    and gushing,
And flapping and rapping and clapping
    and slapping,
And curling and whirling and purling
    and twirling,
And thumping and plumping and bumping
    and jumping,
And dashing and flashing and splashing
    and clashing,
All at once and all o'er, with a mighty uproar,
And this way the Water comes down at Lodore.

—*Robert Southey*

47

The Snow-Queen
HANS CHRISTIAN ANDERSEN

ONCE there was a devilish Hobgoblin. One day he made a mirror which caused all that was good and beautiful, when it was reflected therein, to look poor and mean. The best persons were turned into frights or appeared to stand on their heads. "That's glorious fun!" said the Hobgoblin.

Then all the other Hobgoblins told each other that now only could they see the world as it really looked. And they ran about with the mirror until at last there was not a land or a person that was not represented there twisted all out of shape. Then they flew up into the sky, meaning to have some fun there. But the mirror was now grinning terribly at the malicious joke it was playing. And suddenly it shook so with its grinning that it flew out of the Hobgoblins' hands and fell to the earth where it was dashed in a hundred million pieces. And now it worked much more evil than before, for some of these pieces were hardly as large as a grain of sand. They flew about in the wide world and when they got into peoples' eyes, there they stayed. Then people saw everything distorted or only had an eye for that which was evil. Sometimes someone even got a splinter in his heart and then his heart became a lump of ice. Now we shall hear what happened.

THE MAGIC GARDEN

In a large town, where there were so many houses and so many people that there was no room left for everybody to have a garden, there lived a boy and a girl. They were not brother and sister, but they loved each other just as much as if they were. Their parents lived opposite each other in two attic rooms. The roof of one house just touched the roof of the other with only a rain-water gutter between them. They each had a little dormer window, so one had only to step over the gutter to get from one window to the other. Out on the roof the parents had placed two wooden boxes in which grew pea vines, vegetables, and some little rose trees. And in summer the boy and the girl sat out on the roof among the roses.

In winter it was different. Often the windows were frozen over. But then the two heated copper pennies on the stove and laid the hot pennies on the windowpane. Thus they made capital peepholes through which to look out at each other. The boy's name was Kay, the girl's was Gerda.

One day there was quite a snowstorm. "It is the white bees that are swarming," said Kay's old grandmother.

"Do the white bees choose a queen?" asked Kay, for he knew that the honeybees always have one.

"Yes," said the grandmother. "The Snow-Queen flies where the swarm hangs in the thickest clusters. Many a winter's night she flits through the streets and peeps in at the windows, and then they freeze in wonderful patterns that look like flowers."

That evening Kay made himself a peephole with a heated penny and looked out the window. A few snowflakes were falling and one, the largest of all, remained on the edge of a flower pot. Larger and larger grew that flake of snow. At last it was like a beautiful maiden, dressed in the finest white gauze, made of a million little flakes like stars. She was so lovely, so delicate! But she was of ice, of dazzling, sparkling ice. Her eyes glittered like two stars. She nodded toward the window and beckoned with her hand. Kay was so frightened that he ducked his head below the peephole. But as he did so, he fancied that a great white bird flew away. Then the spring came, the sun shone, green leaves appeared, swallows built their nests, windows were opened, and Kay and Gerda again sat in their garden high up on the roof at the top of the house.

THE MAGIC GARDEN

Gerda had learned a hymn, in which there was something about roses; and she sang it to Kay, who then sang it with her—

The rose in the valley is blooming so sweet,
The Child Jesus is there the children to greet.

And the two were happy singing together out there in the sunshine, with the roses all in bloom about them. But one day Kay cried out suddenly:

"Oh! Something struck me! Struck me sharply! In the heart! And something's got into my eye!"

Gerda threw her arms around his neck. Then he winked and blinked and Gerda looked to see if she could find anything in either of his eyes. But she could see nothing at all.

"I think it is out now," said he, but it was not. It was one of those pieces of glass that had got into his eye—a splinter from the magic mirror that made everything great and good look mean and ugly; and poor Kay had got another piece right in his heart, which began to turn into a lump of ice. And now he looked so strange that Gerda started to cry.

"Why do you cry?" Kay demanded. "You look so ugly when you cry!" Then he looked at the roses. "And those roses! How ugly they are!" he shouted. "That one's worm-eaten! This one's stunted!" And giving the box a kick, he broke off both roses.

"What are you doing?" Gerda cried in alarm. But he did not answer her. Turning away, he ran in at his window and left her there alone.

After that Kay was never the same boy he had been. He started to sneer at people and mimic them. He would get behind his grandmother and mimic her way of speaking. And soon he was able to imitate the gait and manner of everyone in the street. Everything that was peculiar and displeasing in them—that Kay made fun of. It was the glass he had got in his eye, the glass that was sticking in his heart, which made him tease even Gerda, whose soul was devoted to him.

51

One winter day Kay went out with his sled.

"I'm going to the market place to play with the boys!" he bawled to Gerda. And away he went.

In the market place the big boys were hitching their sleds to carts and getting a ride in that way. Kay was enjoying this sport with the rest when all at once a large sleigh appeared in the square. It was painted white, there was some one in it who wore a white fur coat and cap and the horse was white. Twice that sleigh drove round the square. Then Kay tied his sled to it and off he went.

The person who drove turned round to Kay and nodded to him in a friendly manner, just as if they knew each other. So on they went till they came outside the gates of the town. Then the snow began to fall so thickly, that the boy could not see an arm's length before him. Suddenly he got the string he held in his hand in order to get loose from the big sleigh, but it was of no use; his sled hung fast and on he went like the wind. He was quite frightened, and he tried to repeat the Lord's Prayer; but he was only able to remember the multiplication table. The snowflakes grew larger and larger, till they looked like great white birds. Then suddenly the sleigh stopped and the person who drove rose up. It was a lady, tall, slim, and glittering, her cloak and cap of snow. It was the Snow-Queen!

THE MAGIC GARDEN

"It is freezing cold," said she. "Creep in under my coat."
So Kay, enticed, jumped into the sleigh and she wrapped the fur
round him. He felt as though he were sinking into a snowdrift.

"Are you still cold?" she asked, and kissed his forehead. Ah!
the kiss was cold as ice! It went to his very heart, which was
already almost a frozen lump; but, a moment more, and he grew
to like it. He no longer felt the cold that was around him. The
Snow-Queen kissed Kay once more, and then he quite forgot
Gerda, his grandmother, and all whom he had left at his home.

Kay looked at her. She was very beautiful; and she
no longer appeared of ice as before, when she sat outside
the window and beckoned to him. He did not fear
her at all, and told her that he could do
arithmetic sums in his head, and with frac-
tions even; and she smiled while he spoke.
On she flew with him, high over the
black clouds while the storm moaned
and whistled. Beneath them,
the wolves howled,
the snow crackled;
and higher still
the moon
shone, large
and bright.

53

But what became
of Gerda when Kay did
not come home? Where
could he be? Nobody knew. All
the other boys could tell was that
they had seen him tie his sled to a
large and splendid sleigh which drove
down the street and out of the town.
Often, very often, Gerda wept for Kay.

At last spring came with its warm sunshine.

"Maybe Kay fell in the river!" Gerda said.
And she decided that she would go down to the
river and ask it what had become of Kay.

So she put on her new red shoes and went alone to
the river. And she said to the rushing stream, "Is it true that
you have carried away my friend, Kay? I will make you a
present of my red shoes if you will give him back to me."

The blue waves nodded in a strange manner, it seemed to
her, so she took off her red shoes, the most precious things she
possessed, and threw them both into the river. But they fell close to
the bank, and the little waves bore them immediately back to her.

THE MAGIC GARDEN

Gerda thought she had not thrown them out far enough, so she clambered into a boat which lay among the rushes, went to the farthest end, and threw out the shoes again. The boat was not fastened, and her movements made it drift from the shore. She felt it moving and tried to get out, but already it was more than a yard from the land and gliding quickly onward.

Gerda began to cry; but no one heard her except the sparrows. So she sat quite still with only her stockings on. Her red shoes swam behind, but they could not catch the boat; it went so much faster than they.

The banks on both sides were beautiful, with lovely flowers, fine old trees, and slopes dotted with sheep and cows, but not a human being anywhere to be seen. "Perhaps the river will carry me to Kay," said she, and then she grew less sad. Presently she sailed by a large cherry orchard, where stood a little cottage with curious red-and-blue windows. And before it, two wooden soldiers stood sentry, presenting arms when anyone went past.

As the stream drove the boat quite near the land, she called out louder still and then an old woman came out of the cottage, leaning upon a crooked stick. She wore a large broad-brimmed hat which was painted with the most beautiful flowers.

"Poor girl!" said the old Woman; then she caught hold of the boat with her crooked stick, drew it to the bank, and helped Gerda out. "Come and tell me who you are."

When Gerda had told her everything and asked her if she had seen Kay, the Woman answered that he had not passed there yet, but he no doubt would come. Then she took Gerda by the hand, led her into the little cottage, and locked the door. On the table stood the most delicious cherries; and the old Woman let Gerda eat as many as she chose, while she combed her hair with a golden comb so it curled and shone like gold.

"I have often longed for a daughter like you," said the old

THE MAGIC GARDEN

Woman. And while she combed Gerda's hair, the girl forgot her foster-brother Kay more and more, for the old Woman understood magic, and she wanted very much to keep Gerda with her. She therefore went out into the garden and stretched out her crooked stick toward the rosebushes. Beautifully as they were blooming, they all sank into the earth and no one could tell where they had stood. She feared that if Gerda saw the roses, she would remember Kay and run away to seek him.

She now let Gerda into the garden. Oh, what fragrance and what loveliness was there! Gerda knew every flower; but, however many there were, it still seemed to her that one was missing. One day, while she was looking at the old Woman's hat that was painted with flowers, the most beautiful of them all seemed to her to be a rose. The old Woman had forgotten to take the rose from her hat when she made the others vanish in the earth.

"What!" said Gerda. "Are there no roses here?" And she ran about amongst the flower beds and looked, but there was not one to be found. Then she sat down and wept, but her hot tears fell just where a rosebush had sunk; and, when they watered the ground, the tree shot up suddenly fresh and blooming. Gerda kissed the roses, and thought at once of Kay.

"Oh, how long I have stayed! I intended to look for Kay!" And off ran Gerda to the farther end of the garden.

The gate was locked, but she shook the rusted bolt till the gate opened; out she ran in her bare feet. At last she could run no longer, so she sat down on a stone. Then she saw that summer had passed. It was late autumn, though no one would ever have known it in the beautiful garden she had left where there were always flowers and sunshine the whole year round.

"Dear me, how long I have stayed!" said Gerda. "I must not rest any longer." And she sprang up to run on.

At length Gerda had to rest herself again, and there came hopping toward her over the snow a large raven.

57

"Caw! Caw!" He asked her where she was going all alone. So Gerda told him her whole story and asked if he had seen Kay.

The Raven nodded very gravely and said, "It may be—it may be! But now he has forgotten you for the Princess."

"Does he live with a princess?" asked Gerda.

"Yes," said the Raven.

"Oh, won't you take me to the palace?" said Gerda.

So the Raven led Gerda into a garden and, when the lights in the palace had all disappeared, he took her to the back door, which stood half-open. Then they entered the first apartment. Each hall was more magnificent than the other. At last they came into a room where the ceiling was made of great leaves of glass; from this were hung by golden ropes two beds, each shaped like a lily. One was white, and in this lay the Princess; the other was red, and it was here that Gerda hoped to find Kay. She bent back one of the red leaves and saw a brown neck—oh, that was Kay! She called him quite loudly by name. He awoke, turned his head, and—it was not Kay at all! Then out of the white lily leaves the Princess peeped, too, and asked what was the matter. Gerda cried and told them her story.

"Poor girl!" said the Prince and the Princess, and they put Gerda to bed. The next day she was dressed from head to foot in silk and velvet. They offered to let her stay at the palace and lead a happy life, but she would not. She begged to have a carriage with a horse in front, and a pair of shoes, so that she might go forth in the wide world and look for Kay.

Shoes and a muff were given her; and, when she was about to set off, a new carriage drew up before the door. It was of pure gold. And the seats inside it were piled with sugarplums, fruit and gingerbread. The Prince and Princess assisted Gerda into the carriage and wished her all success, while the Raven accompanied her for the first three miles. Then the Raven bade her farewell and flew into a tree.

They drove through the dark wood, but the carriage shone like a torch and caught the eyes of robbers. "It's gold!" cried they! and they rushed forward, seized the horses, knocked down the servants, and pulled Gerda out of the carriage.

"How plump, how beautiful she is! She looks good enough to eat," said an old Robber-woman. Then she drew out a knife, the blade of which shone and glittered.

"Ah," cried her daughter who was very headstrong, "but you shall not touch her. She shall give me her muff and her pretty frock! She shall play with me and sleep in my bed!"

Then the Robber-maiden threw her arms around Gerda and said, "They shall not hurt you as long as I am not displeased with you. You are a princess, aren't you?"

"No," said Gerda; and she then told all that had happened to her, and how much she loved Kay.

The Robber-maiden put both her hands in the handsome muff which was so soft and warm.

"If you are naughty," said she, "no one else shall kill you! I'll do it myself!" And she led Gerda off to the courtyard of the robber's castle. It was full of cracks, and out of the holes ravens and crows were flying; great bulldogs jumped up, but they did not bark for that was forbidden. In the midst of the large, old, smoky hall burned a great fire on the stone floor.

They had something to eat and drink; and then went into a corner, where straw and carpets were lying. Beside them, on laths and perches, sat nearly a hundred pigeons. "They are all mine," said the Robber-maiden. She seized one by the legs and shook it so that its wings fluttered. "Kiss it!" she cried, and flung it in Gerda's face. "And here is my dear old Bac." She dragged a reindeer, that was tied up there, out by the horns. "Every evening I tickle his neck with my sharp knife; it makes him jump about so!" And the Robber-maiden drew forth a long knife and let it glide over the Reindeer's neck. The poor animal kicked, the girl laughed and pulled Gerda into bed with her.

THE MAGIC GARDEN

"Do you intend to keep your knife while you sleep?" asked Gerda, looking sidewise at the knife.

"I always sleep with the knife," said the Robber-maiden. "But tell me once more, all about Kay, and why you have started off into the wide world alone." So Gerda told all again. Then the Robber-maiden wound her arm round Gerda's neck, held the knife in the other hand, and began to snore so loudly that everybody could hear her. But Gerda could not close her eyes. The robbers sat round the fire, sang and drank, and the old Robber-woman jumped about so, that it was outlandish to see her.

Then the Wood-pigeons said, "Coo! coo! we have seen Kay! We saw him in a great white sleigh! He sat by the side of the Snow-Queen. They floated low down over the trees, as we lay in our nest. Coo! coo!"

"Where did the Snow-Queen go?" cried Gerda.

"She is no doubt gone to Lapland where there is always snow and ice. Ask the Reindeer who is tied up here."

"Aye, ice and snow, indeed! There it is glorious and beautiful!" said the Reindeer. "You can run and jump about as you like on those big glittering plains."

In the morning, Gerda told the Robber-maiden all that the Wood-pigeons had said.

"Do you know where Lapland is?" asked she of the Reindeer.

"Who should know better than I?" said the Reindeer. "I was born and bred there on the snowfields."

"Listen," said the Robber-girl to Gerda, "you see that all the robbers are gone. Only my mother is left and she will soon fall asleep. Then I shall do something for you."

When the Robber-woman was having a nap, the Robber-maiden went to the Reindeer and said, "I will untie you so that you may go to Lapland. But you must go quickly, and take this girl to the Snow-Queen, where her friend, Kay, is."

The Reindeer leaped for joy. The Robber-maiden lifted Gerda up and took care to bind her fast on the Reindeer's back. "Here are your worsted leggings, for it will be cold," she said. "The muff I shall keep for myself—it is so very pretty. But here are my mother's great fur gloves." Gerda wept for joy.

"Don't make such faces!" said the Robber-maiden. "Here are two loaves and a ham for you." The bread and the meat were fastened to the Reindeer's back; the Robber-maiden opened the door, called in all the dogs, and then with her knife cut the rope that fastened the Reindeer. "Now off with you," she cried, but take good care of the girl!"

Gerda stretched out her hands with the large fur gloves toward the Robber-maiden, and said, "Farewell!" Then the Reindeer flew on over bush and bramble, through the great wood, over swamps and plains. The wolves howled, the ravens screamed, and the red lights quivered up in the sky.

"Those are my dear old northern lights," said the Reindeer. "Look how they gleam!" And on he sped faster still. Day and night, on he went. The loaves were eaten and the ham, too; and now they were in Lapland.

Suddenly they stopped before a little house, which looked very miserable; the roof reached to the ground and the door was so low that the people had to creep on their hands and knees when they went in or out. Nobody was at home except an old Lapp woman, who was dressing fish by the light of an oil lamp. And the Reindeer told her the whole of Gerda's story.

"Poor thing," said the Lapp woman, "you have far to run still. You have more than a hundred miles to go before you get to Finland; there the Snow-Queen has her country-house, and burns blue lights every evening. I will give you a few words from me, written on a dried fishskin, for paper I have none. This you can take with you to the Finn woman, and she will be able to give you more information than I."

THE MAGIC GARDEN

When Gerda had warmed herself and eaten and drunk, the Lapp woman wrote a few words on a dried fishskin, begged Gerda to take care of them, put her on the Reindeer and bound her fast. Then away sprang the Reindeer. Flicker, flicker blazed the beautiful northern lights; and, at last, they came to Finland. They knocked at the chimney of the Finn woman, for door she had none. There was such a heat inside that the Finn woman, herself, wore very few clothes. She immediately loosened Gerda's clothes and pulled off her gloves and boots for otherwise the heat would have been too great. Then she read and reread what was written on the fishskin. The Reindeer told her Gerda's story at which the Finn woman winked her eyes but said nothing.

"You are so clever," said the Reindeer, "you can, I know, twist all the winds of the world together in a knot. Will you give this maiden a drink that she may possess the strength of twelve men, and overcome the Snow-Queen?"

"The strength of twelve men!" said the Finn woman. "Much good that would do her! 'Tis true Kay is at the Snow-Queen's, he thinks it the best place in the world, but the reason for that is, he has a splinter of glass in his eye and in his heart. These must be got first; otherwise, he will never go back to mankind, and the Snow-Queen will keep her power over him."

"But can you give Gerda nothing to take which will give her power to conquer all this?"

"I can give her no more power than she has already. Don't you see how men and animals are forced to serve her? That power lies in her heart. If she cannot get to the Snow-Queen by herself and rid Kay of the glass, we cannot help her. Two miles from here the garden of the Snow-Queen begins; there you may carry the girl. Set her down by the large bush with red berries, standing in the snow." And now the Finn woman placed Gerda on the Reindeer's back. Off he ran till he came to the bush with red berries; there he set Gerda down.

Gerda ran on
as fast as she could.
A whole regiment of snow-
flakes came rushing against her.
They did not fall from the sky, for it was
quite clear, with the northern lights shining
brightly. These flakes ran along the ground, and
the nearer they came the larger and more terrific
they grew. They were the advance guard of the
Snow-Queen. Some looked like porcupines; others
like bears with hair on end. All were of dazzling
whiteness—all were alive. Gerda began to say the
Lord's Prayer. The cold was so great that her
breath froze as it came out of her mouth and she
could see it like a cloud of smoke in front of her.
It grew thicker and thicker, till it formed
itself into bright little angels, that
grew bigger and bigger
when they lighted
on the earth.

THE MAGIC GARDEN

All had helmets on their heads and spears and shields in their hands; and, when Gerda had finished the Lord's Prayer, she was surrounded by a whole legion of them. They pierced the snow-flakes with their spears, and shivered them into a thousand pieces, so Gerda walked on bravely and in safety through them.

Now we shall see what Kay was doing. He was not thinking of Gerda, least of all that she stood before the palace. The walls of the palace were of driven snow. There were more than a hundred halls, shaped just as the snow had drifted; and all were lit up by the cold, precise northern lights. All were so large, so empty, so icy, and so glittering! Mirth never reigned there; there was never a ball where the white polar bears danced on their hind legs; never a little tea party for the white young lady foxes!

In the middle of the empty, endless hall of snow was a frozen lake cracked in a thousand pieces; and, in the middle of this lake, sat the Snow-Queen when she was at home. Then she said she was sitting on the Mirror of Reason, and that this was the best and only thing in the world to rest on.

Kay was quite blue with cold; but he did not know it, for the Snow-Queen had kissed away his feelings, and his heart was a lump of ice. He was pulling about some sharp, flat pieces of ice, which he laid together in all possible ways, puzzling out how to make something with them. He fitted them into a great many shapes, for they were the "Ice Puzzles of Reason." In his eyes, the figures he made were exceedingly beautiful and of the utmost importance; but this was because of the bit of glass which was still in his eye. Moreover, no matter how many wonderful words he could shape the ice into, the word he wanted most of all, he could never make them spell—that word was "Eternity." The Snow-Queen had said, "If you can shape out that word, you shall be your own master, and I will give you the whole world and a pair of new skates besides." But he could not puzzle it out.

THE MAGIC GARDEN

"I am going now to the warm lands," said the Snow-Queen.
"I must powder my black kettles." (This was what she called
the volcanoes, Vesuvius and Etna.) "It does the lemons and
grapes good." Then away she flew, and Kay sat alone in the
empty halls trying to solve his ice puzzle. There he sat so stiff
and immovable one might have thought him frozen.

Suddenly Gerda stepped through the great portal of cutting
winds into the palace. She repeated her evening prayer, and the
winds dropped as if lulled to sleep. Then she entered the vast,
empty, cold halls. There she beheld Kay and knew him at once.
She flung her arms around his neck, held him fast and cried, "Kay,
dear Kay! Have I found you at last?"

But he sat quite still, stiff and cold. Then Gerda wept hot
tears which fell on his breast, and they thawed his heart and
melted away the bit of the mirror there. He looked at her, and
she sang that song they had often sung together:

The rose in the valley is blooming so sweet,
The Child Jesus is there the children to greet.

At the sound of the song, Kay burst into tears; he wept so much that the last splinter was washed from his eye. Then he cried, "Gerda, dear Gerda! Where have you been so long? And where have I been?" He looked around him. "How cold it is here!" said he. "How empty and cold!" And he clung fast to Gerda, who laughed and wept for joy.

It was such a happy time that even the bits of ice that formed the puzzle on which Kay had been working, began to dance for joy. And when they laid themselves down, lo; they formed exactly the letters the Snow-Queen had told Kay he must find out if he was to become his own master and have the whole world and a pair of new skates. Gerda kissed his cheeks, and they grew rosy; she kissed his eyes, and they shone like her own. Once again he was merry and strong. The Snow-Queen might come back as soon as she liked! There stood his order of release—the word "Eternity" written in letters of ice!

Hand in hand, Kay and Gerda walked off. Together they left the great hall, talking of their mothers and fathers, of their grandmothers, and of the roses on the roof. And wherever they went, the winds were hushed and the sun burst forth.

When they reached the bush with the red berries, they found the Reindeer waiting there for them. He carried them to the Finn woman; she warmed them in her hot room and told them what to do on their journey home. Then the Reindeer took them to the Lapp woman, who made them new clothes and lent them her sledge.

When they reached the country where the first green growing things peeped forth, they took leave of the Reindeer. "Farewell! Farewell!" they cried. Soon they heard the first little birds twittering; and there came out of the wood toward them, riding on a beautiful horse which Gerda knew had once drawn her golden chariot, a young damsel in a bright red cap with pistols at her belt. This was the Robber-maiden who was tired of being at home

and had set out into the world. She and Gerda knew each other at once. It was a joyful meeting.

"You are a nice fellow!" said she to Kay. "I should like to know if you deserve to be run after to the end of the world!"

But Gerda patted her cheeks and told her their story.

"Schnipp-schnapp-schnurre, it's all right at last," said the Robber-maiden; and she took the hands of each and promised that, if she should ever chance to pass through the town where they lived, she would come and pay them a visit. Then away she rode off into the wide, wide world.

Kay and Gerda walked on hand in hand. It was lovely weather, with flowers and greenery everywhere. Soon they recognized the big town where they lived with its tall towers in which the bells still rang their merry peals. They went straight on and hastened up to Kay's grandmother's room, where everything was standing just as they had left it. The clock said,

"Tick! tack!" and the hands moved round. And there were the roses in full bloom at the window. Then suddenly Kay and Gerda understood that they were grown up at last. Yet they sat down in the little chairs on which they had sat as children. And as they did so, all the cold, empty splendor of the Snow-Queen's palace passed from their memories like a bad dream. Kay's grandmother sat in the sunshine and read aloud from the Bible: "Unless ye become as little children, ye cannot enter the kingdom of heaven." Then Kay and Gerda looked in each other's eyes, and all at once they understood the old hymn:

The rose in the valley is blooming so sweet,
The Child Jesus is there the children to greet.

There they sat quite grown up!
And it was summer,
glorious summer!

THE MAGIC GARDEN

THE BELLS

EDGAR ALLAN POE

Hear the sledges with the bells—
Silver bells!
What a world of merriment their melody foretells!
How they tinkle, tinkle, tinkle,
In the icy air of night!
While the stars, that oversprinkle
All the heavens, seem to twinkle
With a crystalline delight;
Keeping time, time, time,
In a sort of Runic rhyme,
To the tin-tin-nab-u-la-tion that so musically wells
From the bells, bells, bells, bells,
Bells, bells, bells—
From the jingling and the tinkling of the bells.

THE SKY AT NIGHT

THE heavens declare the glory of God;
And the firmament sheweth his handywork.

There is one glory of the sun,
And another glory of the moon,
And another glory of the stars;
For one star differeth from
another star in glory.

Praise ye the Lord.
Praise ye the Lord from the heavens:
Praise him in the heights.
Praise ye him, sun and moon:
Praise him, all ye stars
of light.

Both young men and maidens, old men
and children:
Let them praise the name of the Lord.
For his name alone is excellent;
His glory is above the earth
and heaven.

—The Bible

"O Thou Sublime Sweet Evening Star" from Wagner's opera, *Tannhäuser*, has all the peaceful glory of the night sky.

David, the Shepherd Boy*
ARRANGED FROM THE BIBLE

NOW Saul was King in Israel, but Saul did evil. So Samuel, the high priest, came no more to see Saul. Samuel went unto Jesse, the Bethlehemite, to anoint from among his sons one who should be king after Saul's death. And Jesse made seven of his sons to pass before Samuel. And Samuel looked on the eldest, a young man so tall and stately that Samuel said: "Surely the Lord's anointed is before him." But the Lord said unto Samuel, "Look not on his countenance nor on the height of his stature, for the Lord seeth not as man seeth, for man looketh on the outward appearance, but the Lord looketh on the heart."

Then Samuel said unto Jesse, "Are here all thy children?"

And Jesse said: "There remaineth yet the youngest. Behold, he keepeth the sheep!"

And Jesse sent and fetched David, a ruddy lad, fair of face. And the Lord said unto Samuel, "Anoint him, for this is he."

So Samuel took a horn of oil and anointed David to be the king after Saul. Then David returned to his flocks.

*Robert Browning put the story of David playing before Saul in his poem, *Saul*, and the tragic tale of the half-crazy king is the basis of the splendid oratorio, *Saul*, by Händel with its famous funeral march.

And the spirit of the Lord came upon him from that day forward. He looked on the light of the morning when the sky is without a cloud and the whole world seemed to him to skip, to sing, to shout, for joy of God, its Maker.

Then there came a lion and took a lamb out of his flock. And David said, "It is God that girdeth me with strength." And he caught the lion by his beard and slew him and delivered the lamb. And there came a bear likewise and took a lamb. And David smote the bear also and delivered the lamb from his mouth. And God seemed to David like a good shepherd ever guarding his people as a shepherd guardeth his flocks; and he sang in confident trust:

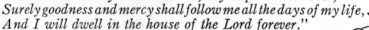

"The Lord is my shepherd, I shall not want;
He maketh me to lie down in green pastures,
He leadeth me beside the still waters;
He restoreth my soul;
He leadeth me in the paths of righteousness for his name's sake.
Yea, though I walk through the Valley of the Shadow of Death,
I will fear no evil; for Thou art with me;
Thy rod and Thy staff they comfort me.
Thou preparest a table before me in the presence of mine enemies;
Thou anointest my head with oil; my cup runneth over;
Surely goodness and mercy shall follow me all the days of my life,
And I will dwell in the house of the Lord forever."

But the spirit of the Lord departed from King Saul, and he was troubled with madness. So his servants said unto him: "Command us to seek out a cunning player upon an harp, for, when the frenzy is on thee, he shall play and thou wilt be well."

Then Saul heard say that David, son of Jesse, played well; so he sent unto Jesse and said: "Send me David, thy son."

And Jesse laded an ass with bread and a bottle of wine and a kid, and sent them by David unto Saul. And when the frenzy was upon Saul, David played before him, fresh and innocent music, full of his trust in God and joy in His creation. So Saul was refreshed and was well and the madness departed from him.

Now in those days the Philistines came against Saul. They stood on a mountain on the one side, and Israel stood on a mountain on the other side, and there was a valley between them.

And there went out a champion of the camp of the Philistines named Goliath, a giant, whose height was six cubits and a span. And he had an helmet of brass on his head and greaves of brass on his legs and he was armed with a coat of mail. And one bearing a shield went before him. And Goliath cried to the armies of Israel morning and evening for forty days, saying: "Choose ye a man that he may come down unto me! If he kill me, then will we be your servants; but, if I kill him, then shall ye be our servants! I defy the armies of Israel this day!"

And Saul and his host were greatly afraid.

Now the three eldest sons of Jesse followed Saul to the battle; therefore, David stayed home to keep his father's sheep. But Jesse said unto David: "Take thou an ephah of corn and ten loaves and run to the camp to look how thy brethern fare. And carry these ten cheeses to the captain of their thousand."

So David went. He came to the place of wagons as the host was going forth, shouting to the battle. Leaving his baggage with the keeper of the baggage, he ran to the army to salute his brethren. And behold there came up the giant, Goliath of Gath; and all the men of Israel fled. But David said, "Who is this Philistine that he should defy the armies of the living God?"

Then Eliab, David's brother, cried: "Why camest thou hither, and with whom hast thou left thy sheep? I know thy pride and the naughtiness of thine heart! Thou art come to see the battle!"

But Saul, hearing how boldly David had spoken, summoned the lad to his tent. And David said unto Saul: "Let no man's heart fail because of this Philistine. Thy servant will go and fight him."

And Saul said unto David: "Thou art not able to go against this Philistine; for thou art but a youth, and he a man of war."

But David said: "The Lord that delivered me out of the paws of a lion and a bear, He will deliver me from this Philistine."

Then Saul said unto David, "Go and the Lord be with thee."

So Saul armed David with his own coat of mail and with his sword; but David said unto Saul, "I cannot go with these, for I have not proved them." And he took them off, and put the sword away, and chose him five smooth stones out of the brook. And he put the stones in his shepherd's bag. And his sling was in his hand. And the Philistine drew near and the man that bore the shield went before him. And Goliath disdained David, because he was but a youth, ruddy and fair of face, and he cursed David by his gods and cried: "Come to me and I will give thy flesh unto the fowls of the air and to the beasts of the field!"

Then said David to the giant: "Thou comest to me with a sword and with a spear and with a shield, but I come to thee in the name of the Lord of Hosts, the God of the armies of Israel whom thou hast defied. This day will the Lord deliver thee into mine hand. And all this assembly shall know that the Lord saveth not with sword and spear, for the battle is the Lord's."

And David ran to meet the Philistine. He put his hand in his bag and took thence a stone and slang it and smote the Philistine in the forehead. And behold, the Philistine fell flat on his face to the earth. And David ran and drew the Philistine's sword and cut off his head. And when the Philistines saw their champion was dead, they arose and fled; and Israel pursued them.

Then Saul was mightily pleased with David. He took the youth that day to dwell in his house. And Saul's son, Jonathan, loved David as his own soul, and he made a covenant with him. He stripped himself of his robes, and of his bow and of his girdle and of his sword, and he gave them to David. Thereafter David went out whithersoever Saul sent him and behaved himself wisely. So Saul set David over his men of war, and all Israel and Judah loved David. But it came to pass when David and Saul returned from battle, that the women came out of all the cities of Israel, singing and dancing to meet them. And the women sang:

"Saul has slain his thousands!"

But then they sang still more joyously, still more loudly:

"And David has slain his ten thousands!"

Then Saul was very wroth and he said: "They have ascribed unto David ten thousands and to me they have ascribed but thousands! What can he have more but the kingdom?"

And Saul eyed David with jealousy from that day forward, and when the madness came on him, he cast a javelin to smite David. But Jonathan pleaded with his father for David, and Michal, Saul's daughter, loved him. So Saul took David back into his favor and gave him Michal to be his wife.

THE MAGIC GARDEN

But in time there was war again and David went out and fought with the Philistines and they fled from him. Then Saul's jealousy returned. He sat sulking, darkly brooding, in his house with his javelin in his hand. And when David came to him in friendship, with all dutiful obedience, Saul sought to smite him even to the wall with the javelin. But David slipped away and Saul smote the javelin into the wall.

Then David fled home to Michal, his wife. But Saul sent messengers unto his house to lie in wait and slay him in the morning. And Michal said unto David, "Save thyself tonight, or tomorrow thou shalt be slain." And Michal let David down through a window and he fled. And Michal took an image of stone and laid it in David's bed and covered it with cloth. And when Saul's messengers came, they found only the image in the bed.

Then Saul was wroth with Jonathan because of his friendship with David, and he cast a javelin at Jonathan, crying: "Thou son of a perverse, rebellious woman! 'Tis to thy hurt that thou hast David for thy friend! For while he liveth thou shalt not be king!" But Jonathan loved David and thought not of himself.

And David returned no more to court, but dwelt in the cave Adullam, and everyone that was in distress, or discontented, or in debt, gathered themselves unto him, about four-hundred in number, and he became captain over them. And David went to the place where was the sword of Goliath, the Philistine, whom he had slain. And he took that sword for his sword.

Then David and his men saved the town of Keilah from the Philistines who robbed the threshing floors. But the very men he had saved sought to betray him. They told Saul that David was in Keilah. So David and his men fled and hid themselves in the wood, in a mountain in the wilderness of Ziph. And Saul sought him every day. But Jonathan went to David to comfort him in the wood. And he said: "Fear not! Thou shalt be king over Israel, and I will be second to thee."

Then the men of Ziph would have delivered David unto Saul; but David went up from thence and dwelt in the wilderness of Engedi. And Saul took three-thousand chosen men and went to seek David on the rocks of the wild goats. And many a time in those days the heart of David was sad and he cried for sorrow: "They that hate me without a cause are more than the hairs of mine head! My God, my God, why hast thou forsaken me!"

Yet his confidence returned in time and he sang in bolder wise:

> *"The Lord is my light and my salvation;*
> *Whom shall I fear?*
> *The Lord is the strength of my life;*
> *Of whom shall I be afraid?*
> *Though an host should encamp against me,*
> *My heart shall not fear."*

THE MAGIC GARDEN

And Saul came to the sheepfolds where was a cave and he went in and lay down. And David and his men were hiding in the innermost parts of the cave. And the men said unto David: "Behold, thine enemy is in thine hands. Do to him as seemest good unto thee." Then David arose and cut off the skirt of Saul's robe. But his heart smote him for what he had done; and he suffered not his servants to rise against Saul, for he cried as Saul went out of the cave: "My Lord, the King."

And when Saul looked back, David said: "Wherefore hearest thou men's words, saying, 'David seekest my hurt'? Look, my father, see! The skirt of thy robe is in my hand. I cut off thy skirt, but killed thee not, and yet thou huntest my life."

Then Saul said: "Is this thy voice, my son David? Thou art more righteous than I, for thou hast rewarded me good for evil." And he lifted up his voice and wept.

But David and his men gat them up again to their strongholds and abode in the wilderness. They lurked in the woods and hid themselves in high hills where was the wild goats' refuge and the crag with the eagles' nest. And they dwelt in caves, companions only to shepherds, who kept their sheep in the wilderness. Neither stole they aught from the shepherds, for they asked their food of rich husbandmen when they held a sheep-shearing feast, or they were fed by some good woman coming with a train of asses, bearing bread and meat, raisins, wine, and figs.

Now in those days, Samuel, the high priest, died. Then Saul came again, following after David as one doth hunt a partridge. But David crept into Saul's camp by night and came where Saul lay sleeping. And he took the spear that stood in the ground by the side of Saul, and the cruse of water at his head. Then he stood on the top of an hill afar off and called:

"Now see where the King's spear is and the cruse of water that was at his head!" And Saul knew David's voice and cried: "I have sinned. Return, my son, David! I will no more do thee harm!"

But David knew Saul meant to kill him. So he fled to the Philistines whom Saul feared. And Saul sought no more for him.

Then the Philistines came again to give battle unto Israel;
and, when Saul saw their host, he was sore afraid. And he disguised himself and went to the Witch of Endor, a woman who
dealt in magic, such an one as God had commanded Saul to put
away out of the land. And Saul bade the Witch to call up the
ghost of Samuel, who was dead, that he might enquire of Samuel
concerning the fate of Israel. And he saw, as it were, the appear-

ance of Samuel, saying: "Tomorrow the
Lord will deliver Israel into the hands of
the Philistines and thou and thy sons shall
die!" Then Saul fell to the earth. There
was no strength left in him.

And the battle went sore against Saul,
and the men of Israel fled. And the Philistines followed hard after Saul, and they
slew Jonathan and the other two sons of
Saul. And the archers hit Saul, and he
was sore wounded. Then said Saul to
his armor-bearer, "Draw thy sword and
thrust me through."

But his armor-bearer would not. So
Saul took a sword and fell upon it. And
when his armor-bearer saw that Saul was
dead, he fell likewise on the sword and
died. And the Philistines found Saul and
his sons fallen in Mount Gilboa. And they
cut off Saul's head and put it in the temple
of Dagon; and they stripped off his armor
and put it in the house of Ashtoreth; and
they fastened his body to the wall of Bethshan.

Now at this time David was off in the desert fighting marauders
who rode swift camels and had burned the city where he lived.
And when he returned in triumph, there came unto him a man who
had escaped from the camp of Saul. And he fell on the earth before
David and cried: "Saul and Jonathan are dead!"

Then David rent his clothes and said: "How are the mighty
fallen! I am distressed for thee, my brother Jonathan. Thy love
to me was wonderful, passing the love of women."

Thereafter David returned to his own homeland. And men
gathered unto him and made him king in place of Saul.

83

Rhodopis and Her Gilded Sandals

The First Cinderella Story*

A Folk Tale of Ancient Egypt

HEAR, O youth! Rho-do′pis, the rosy cheeked, came down through the palm groves to bathe in the river Nile. Beautiful was Rhodopis, lovely as the day-dawn; rosy as clouds of the morning. Her mouth was pure of evil-speaking; her hands were pure of evil-doing; her eyes were clearer than stars. On the brink of the river Rhodopis left her garments and a pair of small gilded sandals. Then she flung herself lightly on the sacred waves of the Nile. But as she disported herself, lo, there came flying toward her a wide-winged, royal eagle. Hovering above the waters, he spied a sudden glistening amid the papyrus reeds. Down to the earth he swooped. He seized one gilded sandal, one beautiful jewelled sandal, and soared again to the heavens. Rhodopis cried aloud. She stretched forth her arms, entreating; but already the eagle was lost to sight in the bright beams of Ra, the sun.

Now it chanced at that very hour, that there sat in the great square of Memphis, before the Temple of Ptah, the young King of the land administering justice and wearing upon his head the crowns of Upper and Lower Egypt. Before him one came dragging a husbandman bound in chains.

"This fellow refuseth his tax!" the tax-collector cried. "He refuseth the tenth of his harvest to thy granaries and to thee!"

The husbandman fell on his face, prostrate before the King.

*The Cinderella story, of which nearly every race has some version, is one of the oldest in the world and unites human nature of all times and climes in the common love of a beautiful fancy. This legend woven about Queen Nitokris, called in the Greek Rhodopis (the rosy cheeked), is probably the oldest. It was told to children several thousand years before Christ, and is to this very day a favorite fairy tale in Egypt.

THE MAGIC GARDEN

"Hail unto thee," he cried, "great Lord of Truth and Justice! Worms destroyed half my wheat; rats laid waste my fields; little birds came and pilfered; hippopotami ate the rest! And when I had naught wherewith to pay thy tax collector, the keepers of the doors of thy granary came and beat me with cudgels. They bound me hand and foot. My wife they cast into chains! My children they left to hunger. Justice, O great King! Justice!"

Then rose up the young King, furious like a panther, glowing as the sun-god. And he cried to the tax-collector:

"My Majesty causes no child of tender age to mourn! My Majesty spoils no woman! Thou shalt serve me no more. Begone!"

And he bade those who held the husbandman to loose him and let him go with a gift to his wife and children.

But he sighed within his breast and unto his own heart he whispered:

"The man is poor, yet doth he, in his poverty, have that which My Majesty lacks, even a wife and children to bring him delight of love." For Pharaoh had found no woman yet worthy to share his throne, worthy to wear on her brow the royal asp of Egypt.

But even as he sighed, there suddenly soared above the square, sweeping in mighty circles, a wide-winged, royal eagle. The eagle hung for a moment poised on the air above, then, lo, from his beak there fell directly into the young King's lap a tiny gilded sandal, a maiden's small jewelled sandal. His Majesty was astounded. He held the trinket forth in the palm of his powerful hand.

"In the name of Isis," he cried, "What maid could wear such footgear, such small and dainty footgear?"

And as he saw in the sandal the marks of the little foot, there rose in his mind a vision of what she must be like who once had worn that sandal,—a tiny, well-made, lovely maid, a lithe and

graceful and willowy maid, a little one like a swift-coursing doe, that bounded over the desert.

"Today My Majesty heareth no more complaints," he cried. Back to the Great House, the Per-o, he went, borne in the royal litter. And he called to his servants and said:

"Haste and bring before me the Chief of the Royal Scribes."

And straightway they brought the Scribe.

And the King said unto the Scribe:

"Thou shalt write me a proclamation."

And the Chief of the Scribes obeyed. And these were the words of the King.

"Let every maid in Egypt try her foot to this sandal; for My Majesty makes decree that she whose foot it fits shall be My Majesty's queen."

THE MAGIC GARDEN

Then the Scribe went forth to the city and a servant bore the sandal on a splendid cushion before him. In squares and public places the Scribe read the King's proclamation, and straightway the ladies came flocking before the throne of the King in the square of the Temple of Ptah, to try on the little sandal. They came in goodly array, high-born maidens and low-born maids, daughters of nobles and daughters of blacksmiths, daughters of glass-blowers, daughters of goldsmiths, daughters of armorers, daughters of potters, daughters of generals, daughters of princes, virgins from Upper Egypt, the Land-of-the-Serpent-goddess, and virgins from Lower Egypt, the realm of Nekhbet, the vulture, but never a one among them, never a single maid in all that vast array, could squeeze her foot into the sandal.

Days passed and days and days. The King was in despair.
His heart grew weary with longing, his heart that was stout as
a lion's.   Again and again he beheld the boat of the sun slowly
rising, mounting the River of Heaven and creeping across the
sky, as with the pace of a snail, and yet the maiden came not.
Nowhere could she be found.   He dreamt of her sleeping and
waking,—a tiny, well-made, lovely maid, a lithe and graceful and
willowy maid, a little one like a swift-coursing doe, that bounded
over the desert.

Then came to the King's Chief Scribe even that very same
husbandman to whom the King had of late forgiven the royal
tax.   And the husbandman said to the Scribe:

"Go to the great Sphinx by the pyramids in the desert. There
cometh each day at daybreak to greet the rising sun, a maid as
lovely as day-dawn, as rosy as clouds of the morning."

The Scribe bore the news to the King and the heart of the
King leapt within him.

"My Majesty goes tomorrow," he said, "to the great Sphinx
of the desert."

In the grayness of early morn, the King and the Scribe set
forth while the first faint beams of Ra crept over the green Nile
valley to the sandy edge of the desert. So they drew near the
Sphinx, where it rose in solemn grandeur out of the yellow sands.
Slowly the red ball of Ra pushed up its topmost rim and a voice
broke out on the stillness, lovely and clear as a bird-song,
greeting the rising sun:—

> *"Thy appearing is beautiful in the horizon of heaven;*
> *Thou fillest all lands with thy beauty.*
> *The birds fly in their haunts,*
> *Their wings adoring thee!"*

And Ra burst forth all at once, flooding the earth with glory,
and touching with sudden light the figure of her who was sing-

ing,—Rhodopis, lovely as daylight, rosy as clouds of the morning. The heart of the King leapt within him. He took from the Scribe the sandal and crossed to the maiden's side, saying:

"Little one, daughter of morning, pray try thy foot to this sandal."

But the maiden bounded away, shy as a doe of the desert, startled as game in the marshes. Twenty paces she ran, then slowly she halted and turned, coming back, half reluctant, half willing. One slender bare foot she put forth while the Great King knelt before her and slipped on the little sandal. And the Great King said to the maiden:

"My Majesty sees in thee the beauty of day at its dawning, the freshness of lotus lilies opening their buds on the water. Thou art as a garden of flowers in the coolness of early breezes. For all the days of my life I would delight in thee. Be thou my wife and my queen."

The maiden's eyes opened wide. She fluttered again as a game-bird. Then sudden her heart was smitten for him who stood there before her, him who was radiant with courage, whose heart was stout as a lion's, who fed upon Truth and Justice.

Shyly she pulled from her girdle the mate to the little sandal and put it upon her foot. Then she placed her hand in the hand of the King saying:

"Thine will I be, great Lord, thou who shinest with strength, whose heart is stout like the lion's! The paths where we walk shall be beautiful because we walk together."

And the King gently kissed her lips and they crossed the desert, hand in hand, unto the city of Memphis, unto the Great House, the Per-o.

Thenceforward by the side of the just and merciful King Rhodopis reigned over Egypt, Rhodopis, lovely as day-dawn, who wore the small gilded sandals.

Phaeton
A Greek Myth

There dwelt once in Greece the nymph Clymene and her son, Phaeton, a bold and headstrong youth. Among his schoolfellows Phaeton once boasted that his father was no common mortal like theirs, but Phoebus Apollo, the mighty Lord of the Sun, who drove across the blue dome of heaven the flaming chariot of day.

"Ho!" laughed his schoolfellows, "words come easy." And they mocked him and scoffed at his boast. "Phoebus seems in no such haste to call thee son as thou art to call him father. For any notice he has ever taken of thee, thou mightest be son of a swineherd."

Then was Phaeton wrathful and stormed back home to his mother.

"These fellows will not believe," he said, "that I am son of Apollo. I shall go to my father and demand that he give me some sign to show them I speak the truth."

"Go, my son," said Clymene. "Thy father will bid thee welcome. But ask of him a modest and moderate sign becoming thy youthful years. Remember he is Lord of the Sun and thou art but a youth."

Phaeton paid little heed to her words. He flung himself out of her presence and was off on his journey. Toward India he travelled, the region of the Sunrise. At length far, far to eastward he came upon the Palace of the Sun. Reared high on splendid columns it stood, ablaze with gold and jewels. Nothing abashed by all its splendor, Phaeton toiled up the steep ascent

*In *Phaeton*, Saint-Saëns imitates, with stringed instruments, wood-winds, and horns, madly galloping horses. The rhythm increases to a terriffic pace until cut short by Jove's thunderbolt, a crash of drums and cymbals.

and entered the halls of the palace. Boldly he pushed on into the very presence of Apollo. But there he was forced to stop, for so bright were the rays streaming from that august head that Phaeton was dazzled by them.

Arrayed in purple robes, Phoebus sat on a throne that glistened as with diamonds. Ranged about him stood the gods and goddesses in charge of the Day, the Month, the Year and the Twenty-four Hours. And behind him stood Spring with garlands of flowers, Summer crowned with ripened grain, Autumn wreathed with purple grapes, and icy Winter coated with frost. Surrounded by these attendants, Apollo beheld the youth and mildly asked him his errand.

"O light of the boundless world!" cried Phaeton. "Phoebus, my father—if thou dost permit me to use that name—I come to be-

There is a fine "Hymn to the Sun" in Rimski-Korsakov's opera, *Le Coq d'Or;* and an old Greek Hymn to Apollo, the sun-god, (3rd Century, B.C.) was discovered in 1893, inscribed on two tablets at Delphi.

seech thee, if I am indeed thy son, give me some proof by which I may be known to the world."

When he ceased speaking, his father laid aside the beams that blinded the boy, held out his arms and bade him approach. Then he held him in a close embrace.

"Thou art indeed my son," said he. "Ask what thou wilt as proof, I solemnly vow to grant thy request."

Phaeton's eyes gleamed. He sprang from his father's arms and flung back his head.

"Grant me that I may drive for one day across the heavens thy mighty chariot of the Sun!"

Then was the father alarmed at such a foolhardy request and repented his rash promise.

"Nay, my Phaeton," he said. "This request only do not make. I beg thee withdraw it. It is not a boon that is safe for thee nor suited at all to thy youth and strength. In thine ignorance thou dost think to attempt what I only am able to do. None but myself may drive the flaming car of day."

"I will have no other boon," cried Phaeton.

"But my son, the first part of the way is so steep my horses, when fresh in the morning, can hardly make the climb. The middle is so high up in the heavens that I myself can scarcely look down without alarm and behold the earth and sea stretched beneath me. The last part of the road descends at a giddy pace so one must know just how to drive to keep from plunging head-long."

Still the obstinate boy insisted. So the father went on:

"Perhaps thou dost think there are splendid palaces and temples to be seen on the way, but ah! on the contrary, the road lies through the midst of frightful monsters—constellations of stars they are called on Earth. Thou must pass by the horns of the Bull, and the gaping jaws of the Lion, between the claws of the Scorpion and the Crab. Nor wilt thou find it easy to guide those fire-breathing horses. I can scarcely hold them myself if they chance to grow unruly. I beg thee to choose more wisely."

"I will have naught but to drive thy car," cried Phaeton.

So at last all unwillingly, Phoebus led the way to where stood the lofty chariot. It was of gold set with shining rows of chrysolites and diamonds. And now while the wilful youth gazed in admiration at the chariot, the Goddess of the Dawn threw open the purple doors of the East, and showed the pathway strewn with roses. Slowly the stars withdrew, led by the Day-star. When he saw the East beginning to glow and the Moon preparing to retire, Phoebus ordered the Hours to harness up the horses. Forth from the lofty stalls they led the steeds, full fed with ambrosia. They harnessed them with jewelled harness and handed Phaeton the reins. Then the father reluctantly set the crown of brilliant rays on his son's head and said with a sad farewell sigh:

"Ah, my son, in this at least heed my advice, spare the whip and hold tight the reins. Thou wilt see the marks of the wheels on the road and they will serve to guide thee."

The agile youth sprang into the chariot, stood erect and grasped the reins with reckless delight.

Meanwhile the horses fill the air with their snortings and fiery breath and stamp the ground, impatient. Now the last bars are let down and the boundless plain of the universe lies open before them. They dart forward, cleave a way through the clouds, and outrun the morning breezes.

Soon the steeds feel that the load they draw is lighter than usual. And now they refuse to obey the reins. They turn from the travelled road. Phaeton is alarmed. He knows not how to guide them. He plies them madly with his whip. Forward they race at breakneck speed.

Phaeton looks down—far down to the earth. His knees shake. In spite of the glare all around him, the sight of his eyes grows dim. He wishes he had never touched his father's horses, never prevailed in his request. He is borne along like a vessel that flies before a tempest, when the pilot can do no more. Much of the heavenly road is left behind but more remains before. He rolls his eyes from the goal whence he began his course to the realms of sunset which he will never reach. He loses his self-command and knows not what to do—whether to draw tight the reins or throw them loose; he forgets the names of the horses. He sees with terror the monstrous forms scattered over the surface of heaven. Here the Scorpion, lashing his ugly tail, stretches crooked claws to snatch him. And when the boy beholds the Scorpion, all his courage fails, he drops the reins from his hands. Now altogether unrestrained, the horses plunge headlong. In among the stars they dash hurling the chariot over pathless places, now up in high heaven, then down, down, down until they are far too close to the earth.

The clouds begin to smoke, the mountain tops take fire, the fields are parched with heat, plants and trees wither, the harvest is ablaze. Great cities burn with their walls and towers.

So Phaeton beholds the world on fire, and feels the heat unbearable. The air he breathes is like a furnace. He dashes forward—he knows not whither. Then the people of Ethiopia were scorched black and the Libyan desert dried up to a waste of burning sand. The Nymphs who dwelt in the fountains mourned the loss of their waters, nor were the rivers safe beneath their banks. The earth cracked open, the sea shrank up. Where before was water appeared dry plains. The fishes sought the lowest depths and the dolphins no longer dared sport as before on the waves. Even Nereus, the old man of the Ocean, and his wife Doris, with the Nereids, their daughters, sought refuge in the deepest caves. Earth, screening her face with her hand, cried out with a husky voice on Jupiter, King of the Heavens, to save her.

Then Jupiter, all powerful, perceiving the ruin wrought by this mad race, mounted the lofty tower whence he sends clouds over the earth and hurls the forked lightnings. Thence he launched a thunderbolt and struck Phaeton from his seat. Headlong, like a shooting star, plunged the youth, his hair ablaze, down, down into the depths of the river Eridanus. And so the earth was saved; showers refreshed her, and she burst again into bloom.

THE CLOUD
PERCY BYSSHE SHELLEY

I bring fresh showers for the thirsting flowers,
    From the seas and the streams;
I bear light shade for the leaves when laid
    In their noonday dreams.
From my wings are shaken the dews that waken
    The sweet buds every one,
When rocked to rest on their mother's breast,
    As she dances about the sun.
I wield the flail of the lashing hail,
    And whiten the green plains under;
And then again I dissolve it in rain,
    And laugh as I pass in thunder.

95

The Prince Who Rode Through
a Mousehole
A Czech Folk Tale

Once there lived a King who had three sons and in time they asked their father's permission to go adventuring into the world.

"My sons," the father answered, "I know 'tis for wives you mean to seek! So be on your way. But return in a year and a day and bring me some gift from your loved ones, that I may know what sort of maidens have pleased you."

Then the Princes decided that each of them would shoot an arrow into the air and start out on his adventures in whatever direction the arrow fell. So they took their crossbows and went to an open field. There the eldest let the bow-string go and his arrow flew to the East. The second let the string go and his arrow flew to the West. But as Yarmil, the youngest, was ready to shoot, a mouse ran past him and into its hole. He let the string go, and his arrow flew after the mouse. At that his brothers jibed:

"Oho! See where thou must go, Yarmil! Into a mousehole!"

"Through a mousehole I shall find fortune, as well as by another way!" Yarmil cried. And when the eldest son rode down the broad and pleasant highway to the East, and the second son down the broad and pleasant highway to the West, Yarmil made straight for the mousehole. He approached it boldly on his horse and when he came full upon it, the small entrance grew suddenly large, so he rode in easily without even slackening speed. Soon he found himself in open country where stood a white marble castle. And scarcely had he entered the gate, when a lady, clad in long, flowing, white robes, came forth to meet him. By the bridle she held a spirited, snow-white steed and she silently beckoned to Yarmil to descend from his horse and mount the one she was holding. As soon as he did so, the horse rose into the air. On and on it flew, till it brought him to earth before a still more splendid castle.

In great amazement Yarmil dismounted but as he took his steed by the bridle to lead him into the courtyard, the horse broke from his hand, rose lightly into the air and disappeared like a great white bird in the clouds. Then Yarmil rapped on the door of the castle. No one answered his summons, but the door itself swung open. So he entered, meeting no living soul. Through ten fine rooms, all ablaze with gold and jewels, he passed. Then he came to an eleventh room where he saw a great crystal tub, and into this tub through a golden pipe, clear, fresh water was pouring. But beyond this room, the last chamber, unlike the others, was small and bare. It contained only a pan, on which diamonds formed these words: "Carry me near your heart and bathe me each day. So you will set free one who is bound."

Still more astonished, Yarmil lifted the diamond cover of the pan, then a golden cover, and lastly a silver one. But at that what should he see at the bottom of the pan save an ugly toad! Yarmil was tempted to run away. But no! in spite of himself he lifted the toad from the pan. At first the touch of it chilled him then he felt strangely happy. Obeying the words on the pan, he took the toad to the room where the crystal tub stood and bathed it with the clear water that flowed from the golden pipes. Then he put it in a pocket of his coat right over his heart.

After that he carried the toad everywhere with him and bathed it faithfully every day. And for all that not a human being ever appeared in the castle, Yarmil passed the year happily enough. Unseen hands served him delicious food, he found books to read and there were gardens to wander in. But as the time drew near when he must return to his father with a present, Yarmil grew sad and anxious. How could he leave the toad? What could he take the King as a gift? But on the very last day of the year, he found on his desk a sheet of paper on which was written:

"Dear Yarmil,—Be patient as I am patient. A gift for thy father thou wilt find in the pan. Give it to him, but tarry not long at home. Put me back in the pan."

So Yarmil, hastening with joy to the pan, found there a splendid casket. This he took and he put the toad carefully back in the pan. Then he hurried to the courtyard. And there the snow-white steed was waiting. As he leapt on its back, it rose up into the air, and flew on and on, till it dropped to earth before the white castle. There the white lady appeared again, gave Yarmil his own horse and took the white one from him. And when he had passed through the gate of the castle and turned to look back, lo! there was naught behind but a

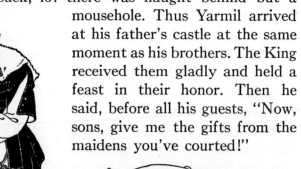

mousehole. Thus Yarmil arrived at his father's castle at the same moment as his brothers. The King received them gladly and held a feast in their honor. Then he said, before all his guests, "Now, sons, give me the gifts from the maidens you've courted!"

THE MAGIC GARDEN

At that the eldest son boasted, "My love is the daughter of a great King! With her I have spent the year in feasting, tourneys and tilts at arms!" And he handed his father a splendid casket.

From it the King took a mirror, about six inches across, and he wondered greatly that in so small a mirror he could see his whole person. Still he said only, "Well, it isn't a bad gift!"

Then the second son also boasted that his love was the daughter of a great King and from his Princess he presented his father with a mirror only four inches across. But the King said again, "It isn't a bad gift!" And he turned to Yarmil, asking, "What has thy Princess sent me?" Silently, Yarmil gave him the casket, for he knew not what was in it. But now the King took from that casket a mirror no bigger than his thumb nail and he cried in amazement: "Why in this tiny mirror I can see not only my whole person but this whole hall, the candles on the walls and all the guests besides! Now here's a Princess who knows what's what!" And he embraced Yarmil warmly. Then he said:

"My sons, return to your Princesses. But come back in a year and a day, and bring me portraits of them!"

With joy the elder brothers promised to obey but Yarmil barely nodded, thinking it might be the portrait of a toad he would have to bring his father. Still he went off through the mousehole again, found the white lady and the white horse and was borne to the castle through the air as before.

Well, the next year passed as the first one had. Yarmil kept the toad in the pocket over his heart and bathed it faithfully every day in the crystal tub. And on the last day of the year he found on his desk a paper on which was written:

"Dear Yarmil! Be patient, as I am patient. Thou hast my portrait in the pan. Give it to thy father but tarry not long. Put me back in the pan."

Then Yarmil found in the pan a casket set with diamonds. Taking it gladly, he put the toad in its place, ran forth, found the white horse and was off for his father's castle. Again the King received his sons with joy and held a great feast for them. Then he asked to see the portraits.

Proudly the eldest brother gave a rich casket to his father. But the King looked at the portrait within it and said, "This lady is pretty enough! Still there are fairer than she in the world!"

Proudly the second son gave his father a still richer casket. But the King looked at the portrait within it, and said again, "This lady is pretty enough! Still there are fairer than she in the world!"

Then he nodded to Yarmil. With trembling hands Yarmil handed his father the diamond casket, for he knew not whether or no it held the portrait of a toad. And he felt no better when he saw his father struck speechless by what was in the casket. But at last the King cried out, "I had not believed in all the world there was such a beautiful maiden!"

And as the guests all came crowding to see the portrait, Yarmil himself looked over his father's shoulder. For the first time he saw the face of his Princess. Such loveliness was unbelievable! Now he regretted no whit that he had spent two years in loneliness, caring patiently for a toad.

The next day the King bade his sons to return again to their Princesses but to bring them back in a year and a day that their

THE MAGIC GARDEN

weddings might be celebrated. So they all went off as before.

When Yarmil reached the splendid castle, he was hoping he would find the beautiful Princess waiting for him. But no! There was only the toad again. So he put the toad back in the pocket over his heart and cared for it as faithfully as ever. This he did until the very last day of the year. Then suddenly he found that the toad had vanished from his pocket. But by this time he had come to have a real affection for the little creature. So he started to search for it everywhere out in the gardens and through all the castle, heading at last for the diamond pan. But when he reached the threshold of the chamber where the pan had been, he stopped as if thunderstruck. For that poor chamber had become the most splendid room in the castle, and in it stood the beautiful maiden of the portrait.

"My dear," she said sweetly, "I am the daughter of a King. A wicked wizard turned me into a toad because I would not marry him. Thou hast endured much for my sake, but now at last thy faithful devotion hath set me free!"

Then she led him out into the courtyard where a carriage with four white horses was waiting. And when the two had entered the carriage, the horses rushed off like the wind. Past the white castle where dwelt the white fairy, who had kept guard over the Princess, and out the gate they went, leaving behind them naught but a mousehole. So they arrived at the King's castle just in the same moment with the two elder brothers and the Princesses they had brought. But, alas! no one ever once looked at them. On Yarmil's bride was every eye fixed. Never had anyone seen so beautiful a maiden. And the King rejoiced most of all at the happiness which had come to his youngest son.

The next day all three weddings were celebrated. Then Yarmil bade his father an affectionate farewell and took his bride back to her father's kingdom where they lived happily ever after.

Vladimir's Adventures in Search of Fortune

A Yugoslavian Tale from Serbia

In days gone by there lived in Serbia a wealthy merchant who had an only son, Vladimir. Now Vladimir was a lad of courage. He would have stood up to the devil himself if he had caught the devil in one of his usual devilish tricks. And he was wise, too, was Vladimir. So the young man's father said to him one day:

"Son, I shall furnish you with a ship and a valuable cargo! Sail with this cargo wherever you like! Trade it where you will! But make yourself rich, Son! Make yourself rich!"

"My Father, I thank you!" Vladimir answered with joy. "Trust me! I'll sail to the best ports for trade! And never fear! I'll make myself rich, Father! Very rich!"

So Vladimir started out with his valuable cargo in high spirits, his head full of visions of mighty fortunes to win. But he had not sailed for many days when he spied, heading toward him, a vessel that flew the Turkish flag. Now the Turks were enemies of the Serbians. Sometimes, too, they were pirates. So Vladimir, placing his men in position for battle and getting his cannon ready, waited, all prepared, expecting the Turkish ship to draw near and fire upon him. But the Turks only sailed quietly past him, paying no heed to him at all. Yet as they passed, Vladimir heard the sound of much weeping and wailing which came from the hold of their ship. Then the mate of Vladimir's vessel said:

"God be praised! The Turks are not interested in us!"

But Vladimir could not get the sound of that weeping and wailing out of his ears. "Hoist all sail!" he commanded the mate. "Put about! Overtake that Turkish vessel!"

So the mate, thinking Vladimir must be out of his senses, hoisted all sail, put about and chased the Turkish ship until they came within hailing distance.

THE MAGIC GARDEN

Swarming with savage Turks that vessel was. But Vladimir called out boldly to the Turkish Captain, "Why does there come such a noise of weeping from your hold?"

In ugly fashion the Turkish Captain leered. "We have a shipload of captives!" he cried. "A shipload of captured Christians! Christians to be sold in the great slave market of Stamboul. 'Tis from them that weeping comes!"

Well, this was no affair of Vladimir's. He should have sailed away on his business of making his fortune. But such grievous, heart-rending weeping and wailing as he heard! And now he heard also the clanking of the captives' chains. And never had he been able from his childhood to pass even a dog in trouble without stopping to give it aid. So he called out loudly, much to the dismay of the mate of his ship:

"You, Captain! What will you take for your shipload of slaves?"

"I'll take all your cargo and nothing less!" The Turkish officer grinned, thinking Vladimir was joking. But at the moment Vladimir was wholly unable to think that that rich cargo of his had been meant by his father to make his fortune. He could think only of the misery of those weeping, wailing slaves. So he cried out impetuously:

"Agreed! I'll give you my whole cargo for those slaves!"

The Turkish Captain gasped. He could hardly believe his ears. But Vladimir started at once having small boats lowered and his cargo loaded, bit by bit, into them. Right there on the high seas, amid the dashing waves, he transferred all his treasures to the Turkish ship. Then when his own vessel had been utterly emptied of its riches, his small boats returned, bringing the captives to him. A sad and sorry lot they were, weakened by hunger, grief and fear, and galled by the chafing of their chains. But Vladimir told them that he would put in to the nearest Christian port, set them ashore and let them all go free to return to their homes. Then they fell with noisy cries of gratitude at his feet.

However, the very last of the captives to appear before him, an old woman and a beautiful young maiden, expressed no such joy at the thought of being set free to go home.

"Great and mighty lord!" the old woman said. "This maiden, Helena, is sole child of a mighty king and I've been her nurse from her infancy. One day we wandered in the garden too far from the palace. There the Turks fell on us and dragged us off as prisoners. But since then we've sailed both weeks and months. We've sailed so far that we could never, never, find our way back home. Pray let us remain with you!"

Then Vladimir was mightily moved with compassion. He set the other slaves ashore but kept Helena and her old nurse with him. And as they sailed over the bounding waves on the journey back to Serbia, he and Helena fell deeply in love with each other. So as soon as they landed they were married. Then Vladimir went home and told his father that he had returned from his venture in search of his fortune with naught save an empty vessel, a penniless maid and a poor old woman to show for his cargo.

"You fool!" his father cried in a fury. "In return for a rich and valuable cargo, you've brought home only two more empty mouths to feed!"

THE MAGIC GARDEN

And with that he bade Vladimir never to darken his door again but to take his young bride and go about his business.

So Vladimir, Helena and the good nurse lived in great poverty for a time. But the two young people loved each other so dearly that even in their poor little hut with naught but hard work and the coarsest of food, they were happy. Only Vladimir sometimes felt a dark blot on the brightness of his joy because he sorrowed over his father's anger. But fathers are fathers. They can't keep anger against their children forever. Moreover, Vladimir's mother was always begging his father to relent. So by-and-by Vladimir's father sent for him and said:

"Son, believe me, I have your interests at heart. You've suffered so much from your first foolish bargain that I'm sure you'll never repeat such folly! So I mean to give you another ship and another cargo as valuable as the first one. Go out again. Trade this merchandise with all your native wit and wisdom! And come back rich, Son! Come back rich!"

Then Vladimir embraced his father and thanked him with tears of joy. And leaving Helena and the old nurse in the care of his father and mother, he set out a second time.

Far, far and afar he sailed. And now he walked his deck and called out orders to his men in a surer, more confident manner than ever, for he was certain that this time he would sell his cargo at a good profit and make himself a fortune.

At last he put into port at a city famous as a center for trade. Going ashore, he set off to see a great merchant, with whom he hoped to make a profitable deal for much of his cargo. But as he was crossing the market place, he saw coming toward him a miserable procession of prisoners, among whom was a white-haired old man, and they were all being driven harshly, cruelly along by a band of soldiers.

"Where are you driving those prisoners?" Vladimir cried.

DONN P. CRANE

"Oh, these!" an officer answered with contempt. "They're just villagers from the country. They couldn't pay the King's taxes! So we're taking them to rot in dungeons!"

Now Vladimir, remembering his father's words, tried to turn away from this pitiful sight of men being thrown into dungeons because they had no money to pay their taxes. He tried, he really tried, to go about his own business. But the desperate look of those prisoners, especially the misery in the eyes of the white-haired old man, continued to haunt him. His feet were on the great merchant's very threshold when he turned away and went instead to the Chief Magistrate of the city.

"How much would it take," he asked the Magistrate, "to pay the debts of those prisoners who are being hauled off to jail because they can't pay their taxes?"

Then the Chief Magistrate consulted his books and announced the sum total owed by all those villagers in taxes. It was an amount equal to the whole value of Vladimir's cargo. But for the life of him Vladimir could not hold back.

"I'll pay their taxes if you'll let them go free!" he cried.

So the Chief Magistrate agreed. And Vladimir delivered all his cargo to him. Gratefully, the prisoners thanked him, in particular the white-haired old man, and they set out with joy for the village from which the soldiers had dragged them.

THE MAGIC GARDEN

But Vladimir was now obliged to go home to his father a second time with an empty ship and not even so much as a copper to show for his cargo.

Well, his father was of course even angrier than before. He sent Vladimir off again with Helena and the nurse. And they lived once more in poverty for months. Moreover, Vladimir had to admit to himself that he hadn't been exactly fair to his father in handing over cargoes bought by his father and not by himself. But however true this was, his father at last relented and called Vladimir to him again.

"Son," he said, "I shall give you one last chance to win yourself a fortune! Another ship and another cargo I'll give you! But this will be the last! Three times is enough!"

Then Vladimir could hardly find words to thank his father. With great joy, he prepared to depart. But this time, to bring him luck, he had fastened to the prow of his ship a large portrait of Helena, his beautiful young wife. And when all was ready he took leave of his loved ones and made off.

Both weeks and months he sailed. At last he dropped anchor in the bay of a great city where dwelt a mighty king. And when the people on the wharf saw the portrait of Helena on the prow of his ship, they began to cry out for admiration of her beauty, while others came swarming down to the shore to see that picture.

Soon the King himself heard about it and came to look at the portrait. But no sooner had he seen it than he grew greatly excited and called for the Captain of the vessel. Then he cried in great agitation to Vladimir, "Stranger, why do you have on the prow of your ship the face of that beautiful maid?"

So Vladimir told him all his tale. Then the King embraced him and cried:

"That maid is my only child! Turks stole her from me! To think she is still alive! God be thanked! O, God be thanked!" And when he had gathered himself together, he took Vladimir to the palace and told the good news to his Queen. After that he proclaimed that Vladimir should be his heir when the time for him to die should come. And the people, having discovered how just, how generous and compassionate Vladimir was, celebrated this announcement with rejoicing and merry festivities everywhere.

Only one person in all the land did not rejoice with the rest. That was the King's Chief Minister, an ugly Prince, who had got himself into so many private quarrels that his face was crisscrossed with scars from wounds which he had received in duels with swords. Now when the Princess was only a child, her father had promised her to Scar-face in marriage. And though he had done nothing in all these years to find her, Scar-face was furious to think that Vladimir had wedded her and would now be King when her father died. And he vowed to himself, "I'll still find means to get this fellow out of my way! I'll still wed the Princess! I'll still inherit the kingdom when the King, her father, dies!"

Meantime, the King gave Vladimir splendid gifts for his mother and father and a much finer ship than his own. Then he said:

"Vladimir, hasten home! Bring my dear daughter Helena back to me as soon as you can! And bring with her, not only her good nurse, but also your mother and father. Your father shall be my brother, your mother my sister!"

"Gladly will I obey you!" Vladimir replied. "But I beg you to send with me one of your Ministers that my father may not disbelieve the strange tale I shall have to tell."

Readily the King agreed to this request. But in utter ignorance of what was in the heart of Scar-face, he assigned to Vladimir as companion this ugly Prince who wanted the Princess for himself!

All through the voyage Scar-face smiled pleasantly and made great pretence of friendship for Vladimir but his heart was dark and he said to himself, "When once I get the girl in my power, I'll make an end of this troublesome fellow!"

In time they reached Vladimir's home port. His father chanced to be down at the shore and seeing his son disembark from such a magnificent ship, he was struck speechless for a time. Then he embraced Vladimir and cried, "Son, Son, Son! You must at last have learned how to make a shrewd bargain!"

But Vladimir smiled and said, "Nay! 'Tis to my first bad bargain that all my good fortune is due!"

And he told his father what had befallen him, while Scar-face stood by to bear witness to the truth of his tale. Then Vladimir went home to Helena. And Helena wept for joy at thought of seeing her father and mother again. So they all set out soon to go to her father's court.

Now Scar-face, having found Helena even lovelier than he had remembered, was still more grimly determined to be rid of her young husband. For weeks they sailed with good weather. Then there came storm and a cloudy black night. Standing in a lonely spot on the heaving deck, Scar-face lifted his voice above the roar of the storm and called out, "Vladimir! Vladimir!"

With no thought of evil, the young man answered the call. But as he drew near, Scar-face sprang on him suddenly, seized him and hurled him overboard into the angry sea before he knew what was happening.

The next morning Helena and Vladimir's parents were in great distress because they could find him nowhere on the ship. Then Scar-face pretended great grief and said:

"Alas and alack! He must have fallen overboard and been lost during the storm last night!" And with that he set himself to comfort the Princess, meaning to win her affections.

Meantime, Vladimir was carried along by the waves and dashed up, bruised and half dead, on a huge, barren rock that stood up alone in a dreary waste of waters. When he came to himself in the morning the storm was over but the sun beat down upon him with merciless heat. Dragging himself to his feet, he looked about for a bush or a tree to shelter him. But no bush or tree grew on that great black rock. He had to count himself fortunate that he found there a kind of moss which he could eat to keep himself alive.

For fifteen days and fifteen nights Vladimir stayed on that rock, scorched by the sun and all but starving. Then at last he saw a small boat coming toward him. Rising, he made frantic signals to it, fearful lest the man in the boat would not come to his aid, for the rock was so jagged and dangerous and the waves beat so fiercely upon it, that landing was well nigh impossible. But as the man drew near enough to see Vladimir's face, lo! he let out a glad cry and waved his hand. Then he made straight toward the dangerous rock, for the man was none other than the white-haired old fellow who had been among the prisoners Vladimir saved from going to jail for failure to pay their taxes. Let the waves beat how they would, the old man steered his boat up to the rock and took Vladimir off safely. Then he rowed to his village where lived those other men whom Vladimir had set free. One and all, they crowded to help him. They gave him food and new clothing.

And now, as Vladimir sat talking with these people in the old man's cottage, he learned that this village was in the realm belonging to Helena's father. So he told them how he was wedded to the Princess of their land and would in time be their King. Then they poured out to him their troubles concerning demands for taxes far larger than they could pay. And he promised to present their case to the King and both now and later, when he himself should be King, to use every effort to see that justice was done to them and everyone else in the land.

After that he went on his way again. But he still had before him a long hard journey afoot. By the time he reached the King's castle his clothes were ragged again, his beard was so long and his face so tanned that the soldiers on guard at the gate did not recognize him. They drove him away with their swords. Just then Vladimir's mother and father, Helena, Scar-face, the King and Queen, came out the gate and saw him. But none of them knew him. Only Helena, seeing the wedding ring on his finger, stopped in great agitation to ask him where he got it.

"That dirty beggar! Don't speak to him!" Scar-face cried. And he hurried her away. But Helena was greatly troubled. When they returned to the palace, she told her father how she had recognized her husband's ring and she urged him to send for the beggar to ask him how he had got it. So the King sent servants to fetch the beggar. And as soon as Helena looked Vladimir full in the face she knew him. Then she cast herself into his arms. Great was the happiness in the household. But Scar-face, in terror of being punished for his crime, stole off into the forest alone and was never heard of more.

As to the people of the country, when they learned of Vladimir's safe return, they rejoiced as never before.

"One day he will be our King!" they cried. "And in him we will have a true friend!"

Then Vladimir's mother said to Vladimir's father:

"After all, was it so fruitless—the way our son sought his fortune?"

The Little-Man-As-Big-As-Your-Thumb-
With-Mustaches-Seven-Miles-Long

A RUSSIAN TALE

ONCE there ruled in Russia a Tsar who had an only son, Ivan. Ivan was a fine lad, skilled in the use of sword and lance and full of wit and wisdom. When he was but a youth he was bolder and braver than any of the Knights at his father's court.

Now one thing only troubled Ivan. His father and mother were always sad and the reason for their sadness he knew well. Before he was born they had had two beautiful little daughters whom they loved so well that they had built for them a white marble palace with turrets of gold. And so anxious had they been for the welfare of these children that they had built a high wall all around the palace that housed them. Furthermore, they had set seventy-seven nurses to watch them indoors, seventy-seven nurses to watch them outdoors and seventy-seven soldiers to guard the gate of their palace. Yet, in spite of all this care, the Tsar and his wife, the Tsaritsa, had one day heard a great noise and commotion. Then the guards and nurses had come running and thrown themselves on the ground before them, crying out in terror:

"Alas! Alas! A whirlwind! A whirlwind blew in through the window of the room where the little Tsarevnas were playing! It snatched them up! It carried them off! It whirled them out the window and off we know not where!"

Then the Tsar and his wife suffered sore affliction, banquets ceased at their court and sad grief sat beside them. Everywhere the Tsar had searched for his daughters but nowhere had he found them. So he had given them up for dead.

Well, now that Ivan was old enough to consider these matters and bold enough to go out and act on any conclusion he reached, he went one day to the Tsar and bowed before him.

"My father," he said, "I think often of my sisters who were lost. And I cannot believe that the whirlwind which carried them off was just an ordinary whirlwind. 'Tis my belief that some evil demon in the form of a whirlwind bore them away. I think they are still alive! So I beg thy consent to search for this demon that I may force him to give my sisters up!"

"Nay, nay!" the Tsar replied. "Thou art too young, my son, to go forth on so dangerous an errand. And thou art mine heir, the Tsarevitch! I cannot risk losing thee as I have lost thy sisters! Yet thy words impress me greatly. I'll summon my Knights! I'll call for a volunteer from among them to go out, seek this demon and deliver my beloved daughters!"

"Thou hast great faith in thy Knights!" Ivan smiled. "But methinks not one of them will volunteer for such dangerous service. Indeed, if any one among them really volunteers to go, I'll give him my rights as heir to thy Tsardom! I'll serve as his scullion! I'll clean his pots and pans!"

However, the Tsar still believed in his Knights. So he called them together and spake to them thus:

"Long have I believed that my daughters were carried off by a whirlwind. But now I'm convinced 'twas a powerful malicious demon, wrapped in a whirlwind, who bore them away. So speak up,

my brave Knights! Who among you will volunteer to go forth,
seek this evil demon and wrest my daughters from him? He who
succeeds in this task shall have to wife whichever of my lovely
daughters he chooses! And with her he shall have half my Tsardom!"

But not a single Knight spoke up. Hiding one behind another,
they all kept silent. This task was far too dangerous. So Ivan said:

"Now thou seest the truth, my father! No one save me is
willing to render thee this service! So give me thy blessing and
let me go!"

"So-be-it!" the Tsar replied with sorrow. "If thou alone art
brave in my Tsardom, thou must go! And I will give thee to take
with thee a hundred thousand soldiers!"

"Nay!" Ivan answered. "I want no soldiers! This is no
affair for soldiers! In this matter one must be quick of wit and
full of wisdom. I shall go forth alone, taking with me only my
wits and my sweet-sounding harp! And if I come not back in
three years, choose another as heir to thy Tsardom!"

Then Ivan took his harp and went on his way. He went and
went near and far and he played on his harp as he went. At last
he came one evening to an opening in a forest. All around were
oak and pine trees lit by the setting sun. And here, within a
railing, stood a strange little house. It was supported on hen's
legs and those legs kept walking, walking, bearing the little house
hither and yon, as though it had been no more than the body of
a hen. At last when Ivan saw that those legs would never keep
still, he spake up and cried:

> *"Turn round, little house, turn round!*
> *I want to come inside!*
> *Let thy back to the forest be found!*
> *Thy door to me open wide!"*

At that the little house stopped walking. It stood as though
eyeing him warily with its questioning little front window.

THE MAGIC GARDEN

Then it turned around, opened its door and Ivan went inside. There he saw sitting an old, old woman, Baba Yaga, the bony one.

"Fie! Fie! Why hast thou come here where no Russian soul ever enters?" cried Baba Yaga.

"Ask me no questions tonight, little Granny," said Ivan. "Morning is wiser than evening! Give me food tonight!"

So Baba Yaga leaped up and prepared him food. Then leaving him in the house, she went out doors to sleep. Well, the night was quiet enough, for the house settled down on the earth like a hen gone to roost. But in the morning Ivan was awakened by being jounced roughly about, for those hen's legs were carrying the hut around again and scratching in the dirt as though they had really belonged to hens. But Ivan jumped out the door and found Baba Yaga under a pine tree. Then he said to her:

"I'm seeking my lost sisters! Dear little Granny, canst thou tell me where I might find them?"

"Aye!" Baba Yaga answered. "They are kept prisoners by the Little-Man-As-Big-As-Your-Thumb-With-Mustaches-Seven-Miles-Long. And a terrible demon is he! His strength is as that of the whirlwind! He can pull up an oak tree by its roots!"

"Be his strength thrice ten times that of a man," said Ivan, "God will not give a Russian soul over to such a swine."

"Well, if thou wouldst risk thy life," said Baba Yaga, "follow the road before my door. It will lead thee to a hut with a garden and a sheepfold. These the Little Man carried off at one swoop from a peasant of the Steppes and there is where he dwells!"

So Ivan thanked Baba Yaga, took his harp and was off. At length he came to the hut with a sheepfold and a garden. And as no one answered his knock at the door, he lifted the latch and walked in. But the Little Man was not in the hut. So Ivan considered how he might bring the demon to him. At length he took the kettle from the fireplace, filled it full of cabbages and other vegetables from the garden and made a savory stew.

No sooner had the odor of that stew begun to drift off on the air than there came a rumbling, a thundering and a snorting as of a storm wind. The door was nearly torn off its hinges and into the room blew the Little-Man-As-Big-As-Your-Thumb-With-Mustaches-Seven-Miles-Long. His mustaches bristled with rage, beneath his beetling brows he frowned at Ivan, and he shrieked in a terrible voice, "How dare you come into my hut? How dare you make stew of my cabbages?"

But Ivan looked at him calmly and said, "You ought to grow a little bigger before you shriek so!"

At that the Little Man fell into a fury. Seizing hold of both door posts, he shook the whole house like a tempest. Then he flung himself violently on Ivan. But though his strength seemed thrice ten times that of Ivan's, Ivan was not afraid, for he knew that the Little Man was in such a tantrum he had no wits left to act with sense.

Dodging well out of the Little Man's reach, Ivan seized him by his long mustaches and held on tight. Then he began to drag him around the hut. The Little Man yanked and pulled, he shouted and roared. At length with a terrible wrench, he jerked himself loose and was off out the door, leaving the ends of his mustaches clutched tight in Ivan's fists.

Ivan made after him but the Little Man flew up in the air and vanished. So Ivan knew no more than before where to search for his sisters. Then he thought a while and decided, "I'll get a boat and ferry people over the nearest river. And I'll ask everyone who crosses where I might find the Little-Man-As-Big-As-Your-Thumb-With-Mustaches-Seven-Miles-Long."

So Ivan took his harp and went to the river. There for a year he ferried people across but not one of them could answer his question. Then at last he ferried over three old men just returned from a pilgrimage to the Holy Land. They offered him gold and jewels to pay for their passage, but Ivan replied, "I want no pay. Tell me, rather, where I may find the Little-Man-As-Big-As-Your-Thumb-With-Mustaches-Seven-Miles-Long."

Then the eldest pilgrim answered, "Friend, thou has but to wish thyself where the Little Man is, and thou wilt be there!"

So Ivan wished to be where the Little Man kept his sisters, and in a twinkling he found himself among gloomy rocks and cliffs by the sea. Near the mouth of a dark, yawning cave in one of the cliffs the Little Man was sitting.

"You! What brings you here?" he screeched as he saw Ivan.

"I've come for my sisters!" Ivan answered.

But the Little Man laughed mockingly. Slipping into the black depths of the cave, he came forth, dragging by their golden hair two lovely maidens whom Ivan knew to be his sisters.

"I'll pitch them in the sea!" the Little Man roared. And he dragged them off toward the foaming waves that came dashing up on the great jagged rocks.

Ivan had to think fast. Seizing his harp, he drew his hands across its strings and struck up a lively tune. And no sooner did the Little Man hear the first strains of that lively, compelling music than he loosed his hold of the maidens and started to dance, as though forcibly obliged to do so. Howling, shrieking, roaring, he spun round and round. He leapt from the ground, he twisted, he turned, he twirled. And his long white mustaches, twisting and twirling with him, formed a spiral about him till he looked like nothing so much as a whirlwind. But for all his rage and his fury he could not stop dancing while that harp played.

So Ivan, setting his harp on the ground, bade it to go on playing of itself. Then leaving the Little Man still howling, shrieking and twirling, he put an arm about each of his sisters and led them away. Thus he delivered them safely to their mother and father who received them with a joy beyond words.

Then Ivan said to the Tsar, "Thou seest, my father, that a hundred thousand soldiers could not have freed my sisters! A hundred thousand soldiers can never equal the power of just one man if that man uses his wits and his wisdom!"

THE MAGIC GARDEN

Columbine and Her Playfellows of the Italian Pantomime*

ONCE there lived in a pink stucco house on the market place in a little village of Italy a cross-grained old fellow named Pantaloon. On the lower floor of his house he had a vegetable shop where he kept his lovely daughter, Columbine, forever selling onions, turnips, lettuces and garlic. But Columbine was a merry creature. When she could get away from the shop, she was always dancing, skipping. For sheer joy she danced, like a sunbeam—here, there, and everywhere. Villagers called as she passed:

> "Haste thee, Nymph, and bring with thee,
> Jest and youthful Jollity
> Come and trip it, as you go,
> On the light fantastic toe."

But Pantaloon, her father, was sober as an owl. He sat in a room full of books, directly above the shop and pored over some huge volume, while Columbine served their customers—

> Dismal, doleful Pantaloon,
> Downcast eyes and shuffle-shoon,
> Up to ears in volumes old,
> Buried deep in must and mould!

Whenever Pantaloon chanced to see Columbine dancing, he shook his cane at her and bade her be prim and sedate. But Columbine did not like always to stay at the shop. Sometimes she ran to the meadows to frisk among kindly shepherd folk who tended their snow-white sheep. But, when she returned from such frolics, Pantaloon

*From early days, a favorite entertainment in many countries, especially at holiday time, has been the pantomime or dumb show in which actors bring out the story by their motions without speaking any words. In Italy, Columbine, Pierrot, and Harlequin became regular characters in the pantomime and from Italy, they spread to England, France, and the rest of the world.

greeted her angrily, tossed her flowers out of the window, threatened her with his cane and set her to work again. And when her work was over, he sent his servant to bring her upstairs, then he set her down primly before him and preached to her with a huge opened book on his knees.

Now Pantaloon's servant was the Clown—

> *Simple Simon, silly goose,*
> *Blockhead, booby, most obtuse!*

Whatever Pantaloon did, the Clown would mimic. While Pantaloon preached to Columbine, the Clown sat humped over a monstrous book and preached to a little white pig.

One day Pantaloon, beside himself with Columbine's friskings, said to the Clown: "Fetch my young neighbor, Pierrot! Bid him to mind Columbine while Columbine minds the shop!

> *To bottle up her spirits,*
> *Put snuffers on her joy,*
> *To bridle, bit, and curb her,*
> *Bring here that pensive boy!"*

So the Clown hitched his pig to a little cart and went riding off to fetch Pierrot.

Now Pierrot was a lovable fellow who had often brought nosegays to Columbine, and he was overjoyed to come and be her companion at Pantaloon's request. But he was quiet and thoughtful, and his garments were white with spots of black, like the moonlight gleam among shadows. Columbine had been longing for a gay play-fellow, but Pierrot sang to her, to the accompaniment of his lute, of the soft, tender beauty of moonlight, of the restful peace of cool shadows and the quiet calm of still waters. And he sang of the nightingale—

> *"Sweet bird, that shunn'st the noise of folly,*
> *Most musical, most melancholy!"*

But Columbine would have nothing to do with shadows or

quiet. Like the sunshine, she was one to twinkle and beam and go dancing everywhere. So Columbine teased poor Pierrot and he found no way to please her.

One day while they tended the shop, and Pantaloon sat in

the room above with his nose in some musty old tome, Columbine hid from Pierrot. He chased her here and there, in and out, in and out, just as the shadows of leaves play hide-and-seek with the sunbeams. Then she slipped away altogether, left him alone to sell onions and whisked away to the woodland.

As she wandered through a beautiful grove of beech trees, she threw back her head and lifted her arms and cried out for a play-fellow. Suddenly the wind came frolicking by, flipped her gauze skirts, tweaked her hair, and snatched off a rose from her bosom. Then it ducked away, swirled around a great tree and bang! there bounced out on the other side a jolly gay fellow in scarlet and yellow, who leaped up high in the air, turned hand-springs, and bounced like a rubber ball. For a moment Columbine held back and knew not what to think, but Harlequin seized her by the hand and then heigho for a frolic! Then for—

> *Quips and Cranks and wanton Wiles,**
> *Nods and Becks and wreathed Smiles,*
> *Sport that wrinkled Care derides,*
> *And Laughter, holding both his sides!*

As Columbine frolicked with Harlequin, the Clown came through the woods, sent out by the angry Pantaloon, to look for his missing daughter. Master Clown looked in the most

impossible places, he bent from his hips with his knees very stiff, and peeped under tiny flowers where not even a grasshopper could have hid, he stretched up his neck like a giraffe's, to look into birds' nests in the trees, and twisted himself into bowknots as he peered everywhere about. What with looking where they could not have been, and never

*This poem, the one on page 123, and the first one on page 119, are from Milton's *L'Allegro*, a beautiful celebration of pure joy. The last poem on page 120, is from *Il Penseroso*, a poem of gentle sadness.

THE MAGIC GARDEN

where they might have been, he backed into Columbine and Harlequin and bumped straight into them. Then he stood on his head, shook his feet in their faces, and went running off on his hands to tell his tale to his master.

Soon, sputtering and angry, shaking his head and his fists, and threatening with his cane, along through the woods came Pantaloon. Leading the way before him, importantly swaggered the Clown.

Columbine and Harlequin were still dancing, laughing, chasing, but they spied the two coming a long way off, and hid behind a tree. When Pantaloon and the Clown were almost upon them, booh! out popped Harlequin, over bowled the two in astonishment, and off danced Harlequin and Columbine. Pantaloon and the Clown picked themselves up and gave chase, but just as they were hot on the heels of the pair, the Clown tripped over a straw and fell, while his master went sprawling on top of him. The chase was long and merry. Pantaloon and the Clown caught a straying donkey and flung themselves both on his back, but the donkey balked, pitched Pantaloon into a rain-barrel and the Clown into a tub of whitewash. So Harlequin and Columbine soon out-distanced their pursuers.

Meantime, Pierrot, left alone, set out sorrowfully to find his beloved Columbine and he played his lute and sang sad songs as he went. At last he came to a country fair, where the shepherd folk were gathered with their sheep. Some had joined in quaint folk dances, while others crowded about the place where tumblers were giving a show. There were—

> —many a youth and many a maid
> Dancing in the chequered shade,
> And young and old come forth to play
> On a sunshine holiday.

In the midst of the crowd, Pierrot spied Columbine and Harlequin. From a shepherd he purchased a tiny white lamb, with a silver bell on a little blue ribbon about its neck.

Music for *L'Allegro* and *Il Penseroso* was written by George Frederick Handel (1685-1759). In *Il Penseroso*, the flute imitates the voice of a bird.

Then he offered the gift to Columbine. Columbine took it and kissed it, but Harlequin began at once to play mischievous pranks on Pierrot. He flipped his clothes, tweaked off his cap, and startled him with sudden dartings. And Columbine joined in the laughter at Pierrot's expense. Seeing how much she seemed to prefer the madcap Harlequin, Pierrot sadly left her. As the days went by, Columbine had less and less time for Pierrot. Harlequin was always popping in at the window and leading her off for a frolic. So, there came a day when Pierrot could endure it no more. He packed his belongings into a bundle, tied the bundle to the end of a stick, sang one last farewell song below Columbine's empty balcony, and set out into the world.

At first, when Columbine found he was gone, she tossed her head and pretended that she did not care at all. She still raced off with Harlequin but, as month after month passed by, she began to miss Pierrot sadly. She grew tired of always frolicking. Without the thoughtful quiet of Pierrot to rest in, she could not enjoy the bounding merriment of Harlequin. Her feet began to stop twinkling and she left off skipping and dancing. Then Pantaloon was content. He thought he had quenched forever the bubbling spring of her joy.

But, in time, there came to the village the fame of a certain poet, who wrote most beautiful plays and of whom all Italy spoke. One day, a stage was set up in one corner of the market place. A play by the famous poet was to be given there. Harlequin and Columbine joined the crowd around the stage. At last the play began. Columbine's heart beat fast, for there, on the stage, appeared a twinkling little maid who was the image of herself. And there was

Harlequin, yes, there was Pierrot, too! The play told how much Pierrot had loved his Columbine, and how Columbine had deserted him to play all day with Harlequin. The Columbine and Harlequin were only an actor and actress, but, when Pierrot began to sing— ah! Columbine knew the truth! That was Pierrot, himself!

He sang of the loneliness of the world, the sadness in his heart, and his longing for Columbine. He sang till Columbine wept. Yes, Pierrot was the poet who had written the play! When the play was over, Columbine held out her hands, Pierrot sprang from the stage, and Columbine asked his forgiveness. In her joy at seeing him again, she forgot all about Harlequin and, hand in hand with Pierrot, she ran off into the meadows.

When Pierrot and Columbine came back to Pantaloon's shop, they made it into a flower shop. They turned out the onions and turnips, the lettuces and garlic, and filled it full of flowers.

Pantaloon grumbled and stormed, but, when he knew that Columbine had chosen Pierrot to be her companion forever, he was quite content. He preached no more to her but to the Clown and his little pet pig.

The Six Swans
A German Fairy Tale

Once upon a time a King went a-hunting in a great wood, and he pursued a wild boar so eagerly that none of his people could follow him. Never once did he stop to look about him until nightfall, and then he found he had quite lost his way. As he was searching for a path, he suddenly saw before him an ugly old woman, and she was a witch, though the King did not know it.

"Good dame," said the King, "can you show me the way out of the wood?"

"Oh, yes, my lord King," she answered, "but on one condition, and if you do not fulfill it, you shall never get home again."

"What is the condition?" asked the King.

"I have a daughter," said the old dame, "as fair as any in the world, and if you will promise to make her your Queen, then and then only will I lead you safely out of the forest."

Well, the King was in such a fix, he knew not what else to do, so he consented, and the old witch led him straight off to her hut. There sat her daughter by the fire, but though she was very beautiful, she did not please the King. He could not even look at her without an inward shudder. Nevertheless, as he had promised, he took her before him on his horse, the old woman showed him the way, and soon he was safely back in his castle.

Now the King had been married before and already had seven beautiful children whom he loved better than all the world, but he knew well enough that this strange new Queen would be only too likely to do them some mischief; so he took them secretly and hid them away in a lonely castle deep in the midst of a wood. The road to this place was so hard to find, that the King himself would never have found it, had it not been for a certain clew of yarn that unrolled itself when he threw it down before him and showed him the way through the forest.

THE MAGIC GARDEN

Time passed and the King went so often to see his six sons and one daughter that the Queen grew very curious to know where he went so often alone. So she gave herself no rest until she discovered the secret of the clew. Then she made some white shirts for the boys and sewed in each one a charm she had learned from her mother. And when the King next rode off a-hunting, she took the shirts and the ball of yarn and went secretly into the forest. Sure enough the yarn showed her the way and there she came to the hidden castle. Seeing someone coming in the distance, the boys, who were now nearly grown up, thought it was their father and ran joyously to meet him. But the wicked witch threw over each as he drew near, one of the shirts, and immediately they were no longer youths, but changed into swans, that mounted up into the air and flew, soaring over the tree-tops. Then the Queen went home laughing hideously to think she was rid of the King's sons forever.

But she knew nothing about the King's one daughter, for the maiden had not run out with her brothers. She had seen what had happened from the window, and all day long she went sorrowfully about, picking up the feathers that had dropped from her brothers' wings in the courtyard. But when night came on, she said to herself, "I must stay here no longer. I shall go and seek for my brothers."

So she fled away farther still into the wood. She went on all that night and the next day until she could go no longer for weariness. At last she saw a rude hut before her. In she went and found there a room with six beds, and six chairs, and six plates and knives on the table. So she guessed that this might be the place where her brothers were staying, and she crept under one of the beds to wait and see what would happen.

When it was near the time of sun-setting, she heard a rustling sound and behold! six handsome white swans came flying in at the window. They alighted on the ground and blew at one another until they had blown all their feathers off; then they stripped off their swan-skins as though they had been shirts. The maiden knew them at once for her brothers and crept gladly from under the bed. The brothers, too, were overjoyed to see their sister, but even as they embraced her, they cried:

"Alas! we can only stay with you one little quarter of an hour. For that length of time every evening we keep our human shapes, but after that we are changed again into swans."

"Can nothing be done to free you?" cried their sister, weeping.

"Oh, no!" they replied. "The work would be too hard for you. For six whole years you would be obliged never to speak or laugh, and you would have, during that time, to spin, weave

and make six shirts out of aster-down gathered by night. If you failed in any of these things, all would be lost."

Just as the brothers finished speaking, the quarter of an hour came to an end, they changed into swans and flew out of the window. At this, the maiden made up her mind on the spot to set her brothers free, no matter what it might cost her. So she stayed and kept house for her brothers. She kept their beds clean and white; she fetched the wood and the vegetables; she watched the pot on the fire that their supper might be ready and she was always down by the shore of a nearby pond when they came home at sunset. For a quarter of an hour after that they would be her brothers, then off they must fly again as white swans. But, though she made them so comfortable, the Princess never spoke a word to them or laughed one little laugh. And by moonlight and starlight she was always out gathering down. No matter how lonely seemed the dark forest, nor how black the shadows, she was always gathering down.

When she had been going on like this for a long, long time, the King of the country where she now lived went hunting one day. But he got separated from his companions and was wandering about at nightfall all alone, when whom should he see sitting up in a tree and carding her down, but a beautiful maiden.

"Who art thou?" asked the King, struck with her loveliness.

She answered him not a word.

"What art thou doing up in that tree?"

She answered him not a word. He spoke to her in all the languages he knew, but still she answered him never a word. The King, however, felt a very great love for her rise in his breast, so he climbed the tree, brought her down, cast his mantel about her, set her up on the horse before him, and started off toward the castle. But the maiden wrung her hands and pointed back to her bags full of aster-down. So the King, seeing she wished to have them with her, returned and got them, put them also up on his horse and galloped away once more.

When they reached the castle, the King caused the maiden to be clad in rich garments, and her beauty shone as bright as the morning, but still not a single word would she utter. Her modesty and gentleness so pleased the King that he chose her for his wife and would have no other in all the world. Accordingly, they were married. But it happened that there dwelt with the King as head of his household, a wicked old dame, who wanted no handsome new queen in the castle to take the management out of her hands, so she began at once to speak ill of her.

"Who knows where the maid can have come from?" she said, "and dumb as a door-post, too! She is probably some beggar maid who has stolen the heart of the King!"

To all this evil-speaking the Queen made no answer whatever. No matter how cruel or untrue the words of the old woman were, she never once opened her lips. Sometimes the King begged her to speak with loving words and endearments, but, though her heart longed to reply, she answered never a word. Always she was spinning and weaving her aster-down, cutting and making her shirts.

Year after year went by, till at last the old woman began to whisper and tell abroad that the sweet young queen was a witch who had cast a spell over the King. Now the people could not understand the silent Queen who was always at work and would speak no word, nor stop to join in their festivities, so at last, aroused by the wicked old dame, they went to the King in a mass, proclaimed her a witch and demanded that she be burnt at the stake. Then the King was so sad that there was no end to his sadness, for he still loved his wife very dearly, but the Queen never spoke a word to save herself, so the people seized her out of the castle and dragged her off to the stake.

THE MAGIC GARDEN

Now when all this happened, it was the very last day of the six years during which she had neither spoken nor laughed in order to free her brothers. The six shirts were ready, all except one that wanted a sleeve. When she was dragged to the stake, the Queen carried the six shirts on her arm, but just as she mounted the pile of fagots, and the fire was about to be kindled, she cried out aloud, for there, through the air flying toward her, came six beautiful snow-white swans. With rushing wings they flew and dropped in a circle about her. Quickly she threw the shirts over their heads. Then off dropped their swan skins and her brothers stood safe and sound before her. Only, as one shirt wanted the left sleeve, her youngest brother had a swan's wing instead of a left arm. While the King looked on in astonishment, the brothers and sister embraced and kissed each other. Then the Queen went up to the King and said:

"Dearest husband, now I may dare to speak and tell you I am innocent!" So she told all her tale and the King was over-joyed, while the people fell at her feet and begged her forgiveness.

After that the Queen sent for her dearly loved father to visit her. Then her father saw that the wicked old dame was the very witch who had made him marry her daughter and taught the daughter the charm by means of which she had turned his sons into swans. So he forced her, with the threat of being burned at the stake herself, to take the swan's wing from his youngest son and restore to him his left arm. Then he turned her and her daughter out into the forest alone. But as for the others they all lived happily ever after.

THE ACORN AND THE PUMPKIN
LA FONTAINE

God's works are good.   To prove this truth
I need not search the world, forsooth!
I do it by the nearest Pumpkin!

"Fie! fruit so large on vine so small!"
Exclaimed one day a wise young bumpkin!
"What could He mean who made us all?
This Pumpkin here is out of place.

If I had ordered in this case,
Upon that oak it should have hung—
A noble fruit as ever swung
To grace a tree so firm and strong.

132

THE MAGIC GARDEN

Indeed there's been a great mistake!
Had my opinion but been sought,
When God set out the world to make,
All things had then been as they ought!
All things had then in order come!
This Acorn for example,
No bigger than my thumb,
Had not disgraced a tree so ample.

The more I think, the more I wonder!
The Pumpkin on the oak should grow,
The Acorn on the vine below;
God surely made an awful blunder!"

With such reflections proudly fraught,
Our Sage grew tired of mighty thought,
And threw himself on Nature's lap,
Beneath an oak, to take a nap.

It chanced that during his repose,
An Acorn fell plump on his nose!
He wakened with a mighty start;
He shrieked and seized the injured part!

"Oh! Oh! alas! I bleed! I bleed!
This Acorn 'twas that did the deed!
I see that God had reasons good,
And all His works were understood,
For, truly, what had been my woes,
Had, then, a Pumpkin whacked my nose!"
Thus home he went in humbler mood!

The Golden Bird

A German Fairy Tale

IN olden time there lived a King, who had behind his palace a beautiful garden in which there was a tree that bore golden apples. One day when the apples were nearly ripe, the King had them counted, but on the very next morning one was missing. So the King ordered that a watch should be kept every night beneath the tree.

Now the King had three sons and he ordered the eldest to keep watch first. So the eldest went to the garden. But by midnight he was so sleepy he couldn't keep awake. He let himself go to sleep and next morning another apple was gone.

The following night the second son kept watch. But he couldn't keep awake either. By twelve o'clock he had fallen asleep and in the morning a third golden apple was missing.

Now it came the turn of the youngest son to watch and he was eager to stand guard over the apples. But his father said:

"What use will you be? You're so young you'll be of less use even than your brothers!"

Nevertheless, he let his youngest son go. And this youth kept awake, wide awake. At midnight he was still watching at his post. Then something came rustling through the air. In the moonlight he saw it. What was it? It was shining! It was a bird, a golden bird! Alighting on the apple tree, the Bird plucked off a golden apple. Then the youth shot an arrow at it and the Bird flew away. But the arrow had knocked one of its golden feathers to the earth. So the youth picked it up. Next morning he took it to the King and reported what he had seen.

Then the King cried:

"The rascal that carries off my apples is the Golden Bird, which was stolen long ago from my garden. He must be found and restored to me."

THE MAGIC GARDEN

So he sent his eldest son out to find the Golden Bird. Very clever this youth thought himself. "'Twill take me no time to find that Golden Bird!" he boasted.

Well, he hadn't gone far when he saw a fox sitting at the edge of a wood. So he cocked his gun and took aim at the Fox.

"Don't shoot me!" cried the Fox. "I can give you good counsel! You're seeking the Golden Bird! I'll help you! By evening you'll reach a village which has two inns! One will be brightly lighted and seem very fine and gay! But don't enter there! Go rather to the other inn though it may seem poor and plain!"

"How should a silly beast like you give advice to a clever fellow like me?" the King's son cried. And pulling the trigger of his gun, he shot at the Fox. But he missed it. Then the Fox ran quickly into the wood.

So the King's son went on his way. By evening he came to the village where the two inns were. In one all the lights were lit and there was singing and dancing within, but the other inn looked poor and plain.

"I'd be a fool," he thought, "if I were to go into the shabby inn and pass the good one by!" So he went into the brightly lighted place. After that he lived there in pleasure and reveling, forgetting the Bird, his father and all good counsel.

Well, when months passed by and the eldest did not come home, the second son set out to find the Golden Bird. And the Fox met him as he had the eldest, giving him the same good advice. But the second brother likewise paid no heed to his counsel. Reaching the village with the two inns, he came first on the brightly lighted one. And through a window he saw his brother having a fine time within. So he went in and joined his brother. And from then on those two lived for pleasure only, forgetting the Bird and all good counsel.

Again months passed. Then the King's youngest son wanted to set off to find the Bird. But his father said:

"How should a youngster like you find the Golden Bird when his elder brothers have failed?" However, as the lad continued to urge him, the father finally let him go. Then this lad also met the Fox and heard his good advice. Being modest, good-natured and willing to take good counsel, he said to the Fox, "Be easy, little Fox, I'll do you no harm! I'll follow your advice."

"You shall not repent it," answered the Fox. "And that you may get on more quickly, get up behind on my tail." So the King's son seated himself on the Fox's tail and the Fox ran off with him over stock and stone till his hair whistled in the wind. When they came to the village the youth got off. Then, following the Fox's advice, he passed the brightly lighted inn, turned into the plain one and spent the night there.

The next morning he walked out into the country alone. But he had not gone very far when he found the Fox by the roadside.

"Go straight ahead," said the Fox. "Soon you'll come to the castle where lives the King who has your father's Golden Bird. Before the castle lies a regiment of soldiers. But don't be concerned about them! They'll all be asleep and snoring! Go straight through the midst of them into the castle. Then go through all the rooms. At last you'll come to a chamber where the Golden Bird sits in a plain wooden cage. Close by, will be an empty gold cage which is very splendid. But that cage is all for show. Don't take the Bird out of the plain cage and put it into the fine one or things will go badly for you."

Then the Fox again stretched out his tail, the King's son seated himself upon it and away he went over stock and stone till his hair whistled in the wind.

THE MAGIC GARDEN

When he came to the castle, it was just as the Fox had said. He found the soldiers snoring, walked through the midst of them and on to the room where he saw the Golden Bird. The Bird was in a plain, wooden cage, near it lay the golden apples, and not far off stood the splendid golden cage. Then as the young Prince looked at that magnificent cage, he thought:

"'Twould not be fair to so fine a bird to leave it in the common, ugly cage."

So he opened the door, laid hold of the Bird and put it into the golden cage. But at that moment the Bird uttered a shrill, piercing cry. Then the soldiers awoke, rushed in, seized the youth and dragged him off to prison. The next morning he was taken before the King of that country and sentenced to death. However, the King said to him:

"I'll grant thee thy life if thou wilt bring me the Golden Horse which runs faster than the wind. And if thou canst bring me that horse, I'll give thee in return the Golden Bird!"

So the King's son set off, very downcast. For how was he ever to find the Golden Horse? But all at once, he saw his old friend, the Fox, sitting in the middle of the road.

"Look you," said the Fox, "this has happened because you did not give heed to my good advice! But take courage! I'll help you again! I'll tell you how to get the Golden Horse!"

At this, the King's son rejoiced, promising once more to accept his good counsel and obey it.

"Go straight on!" said the Fox. "Soon you'll come to a castle. There in the stable stands the Golden Horse. Fifty grooms will be lying in front of the stable but they'll be asleep and snoring! Quietly, you can lead the Golden Horse out past them! But of one thing you must take heed—put on the Horse the plain saddle of wood and not the golden one, which hangs close by!"

Then the Fox stretched out his tail, the King's son seated himself upon it and away he went over stock and stone till his hair whistled in the wind.

Everything happened just as the Fox had said. The Prince passed the snoring grooms and found the Golden Horse in the stable. But just as he was about to put the plain saddle on him, he thought, "'Twould shame so beautiful a beast, if I did not give him the splendid saddle which is his by right!"

So he flung the golden saddle over the Horse's back. Scarcely had he done so when the Horse began to neigh loudly. Then the grooms awoke, seized the youth and threw him into prison. The next morning, the King of this country sentenced him to death. However, the King said, "I'll grant thee thy life, young man, and the Golden Horse as well, if thou wilt bring me the Beautiful Princess from the Golden Castle. I'd have her for my bride, but her guardian keeps her from me!"

With a heavy heart the youth set out, not knowing what to do next. But soon he found the trusty Fox again.

"I ought to leave you to the consequences of your folly and disobedience to my good advice!" said the Fox. "But I pity you and I'll help you again! This road leads straight to the Golden Castle. By eventide you'll reach it! And at midnight when everything is quiet, the Beautiful Princess goes alone from the castle to the bathing house in the castle yard. Run up to her at that moment and give her a kiss. Then she will wish to follow you wherever you would take her! Only remember this—do not allow her to take leave of anyone in the castle!"

Then the Fox stretched out his tail, the King's son seated himself upon it and away he went over stock and stone till his hair whistled in the wind.

When he reached the Golden Castle, it was just as the Fox had said. He waited until midnight when everything lay in deep sleep and the Beautiful Princess was going to the bathing house. Then he sprang out and gave her a kiss. She said at once that she would like to go anywhere with him, but she begged him pitifully and with tears to let her take leave of the King of the Golden Castle, who was her guardian. At first he withstood her request, but when she begged more and more earnestly he gave in at last. Well, no sooner had the maiden awakened the King than everyone else in the castle also awoke. Then the youth was laid hold of and cast into prison.

"You may have the Beautiful Princess only if you take away the hill which shuts off the view from my windows!" said the King. "And you must finish your work within eight days!"

So the King's son started digging. For seven days and six nights he dug without once leaving off. But the hill still looked as big as ever. By evening of the seventh day he was sorely discouraged when the Fox appeared again and said:

"You do not deserve that I should take any more trouble about you. Nevertheless, you have faithfully tried to fulfill your task. So lie down to sleep, I'll finish it for you."

Then the young Prince lay down and slept and when he looked out his window next morning, behold, the hill was gone. Running joyously to the King, he reported that his task was fulfilled. So the King had to keep his promise and give him the Beautiful Princess.

Then the King's son and the Princess set forth together and it was not long before the trusty Fox came up with them. Feeling very sad at what he had to say, the King's son now told the Princess he was taking her to wed the King who had the Golden Horse. But the Beautiful Princess wept.

"That doddering old fellow!" she cried. "I don't wish to wed him! I want to go where you go! Besides, the Golden Horse doesn't belong to him! It's mine! He stole it from me!"

Then the Fox said, "If the Princess chooses you, yours she must be. Go now and recover for her the Golden Horse."

"But how can I, one man alone, wrest the Horse from that rascally old King who has fifty grooms to guard his stable?" the King's son demanded.

"Just take the Princess to him," the Fox replied. "Thinking he has her in his power at last, he'll rejoice and have her Golden Horse led forth in exchange. Then mount it quickly, swing the Princess up on the saddle before you and gallop away. No one will ever be able to overtake the Golden Horse!"

Well, all was brought to pass successfully as the Fox had advised. In spite of the fifty grooms, the King's son got the Golden Horse and carried the Princess off. Then the Fox said:

"Now leave the Princess in my care and I'll tell you how to recover your father's Golden Bird from the castle with the regiment of soldiers. Ride boldly into the courtyard. The King means to have a fine procession to show off his power and all the magnificence of his riches. So his soldiers will be lined up for parade. And at their head will be one who carries the Golden Bird in a cage! Swoop down on that man swiftly! Seize the cage and gallop back to us like the wind."

Well, this plan succeeded, too. The King's son found the procession lined up, seized the Golden Bird and returned to the Fox, rejoicing. Then the Fox said:

THE MAGIC GARDEN

"Thus far you've met with success. Yet before I leave you, I'd give you one last piece of advice. Be careful about two things. Don't pay money to buy any thief or other criminal off from his punishment and don't sit on the edge of any well." Then he ran off into the wood while the Prince rode on with the Princess, the Golden Bird and the Golden Horse.

By-and-by he came to the village where his two brothers had remained. Seeing the people there in a great stir of excitement, he asked what the commotion was all about.

"Two thieves are to be hanged!" a man replied.

Then what should the young Prince see but his two brothers being led to the gallows because of crimes they had committed against the people! At once he began to think he'd like to get his brothers off from their punishment. So he stopped and asked a magistrate how he might do so.

"If you pay for the damage they've done, they may go free," the magistrate answered. "But why waste your money on wicked men who have not repented the evil they've done?"

But the King's son did not think twice about it. He paid for his brothers and when they were free, they all went on their way together. Soon they came to the wood where the Fox had first met them. The sun had been shining hotly on them but within the wood it was cool and the brothers, seeing a well there, cried:

"Let us rest by the well and eat and drink!" So the Prince, forgetting once more the Fox's counsel, sat down on the edge of the well. At once the two brothers fell on him and threw him backward into the well. Then they took the Princess, the Horse, and the Bird, and went home to their father.

"We bring you not only your Golden Bird!" they said. "For we have won also the Golden Horse and the Princess from the Golden Castle." And they threatened the Princess with death if she told the truth. So the King believed their tale and rejoiced greatly. But the Horse would not eat, the Bird would not sing, and the Princess sat and wept.

Meantime, it happened that the well into which they had cast the youngest brother was dry, so he fell on soft moss without being hurt at all. But he could not get out again. Yet even in this strait the faithful Fox did not desert him.

THE MAGIC GARDEN

Appearing suddenly, the Fox leapt down to him in the pit.

"Once again by your folly, by forgetting to heed my advice, you've forfeited all right to my help," said the Fox. "Yet I'll give you one more chance to follow my counsel. Your brothers have surrounded this wood with men who are to kill you if you ever get out of this well. So you must change clothes with the woodcutter up there by the roadside. Then no one will recognize you! You can pass safely by the men your brothers have set to catch you. But mind this! You must continue to wear the poor clothes of the woodcutter. Don't exchange them for fine ones till you're safe in your father's presence."

Then the Fox bade the Prince grasp his tail and keep tight hold of it and so he pulled him up out of the well. There the youth exchanged his good clothes for the ragged ones of the woodcutter. Thus he arrived in safety at his father's castle. But there he longed to exchange his poor clothes for fine ones before he entered the presence of his father and the Princess. However, he remembered the Fox's wise counsel and obeyed it. So no one knew who he was and the elder brothers never even dreamed that he was in the castle. But all of a sudden the Bird began to sing, the Horse began to eat and the Princess left off weeping.

"I'm so happy," she said. "I feel as if my true bridegroom had come!" And though she had not yet seen the Prince, she grew so full of courage that she told the King the whole story of what the elder brothers had done.

At once the King commanded that everyone in his castle should be brought before him. And amongst those who came was the Prince in his ragged clothes. But the Princess knew him immediately and threw her arms about him. Then the King, recognizing him also, greeted him gladly. After that the King sent his wicked sons out of his Kingdom to think matters over. But his youngest son married the Princess and lived happily ever after!

WHITE HORSES*

HAMISH HENDRY

I saw them plunging through the foam,
  I saw them prancing up the shore—
A thousand horses, row on row,
  And then a thousand more!

In joy they leaped upon the land,
  In joy they fled before the wind,
Prancing and plunging on they raced,
  The huntsman raced behind.

When this old huntsman goes to sleep,
  The horses live beneath the waves;
They live at peace, and rest in peace,
  Deep in their sea green caves.

But when they hear the huntsman's shout
  Urging his hounds across the sea,
Out from their caves in frenzied fear
  The great white horses flee!

Today they plunged right through the foam,
  Today they pranced right up the shore,
A thousand horses, row on row,
  And then a thousand more.

*Used by permission of the publishers, G. P. Putnam's Sons.

BABE RUTH, the HOME-RUN KING of BASEBALL

Not all the kings in the world have lived in castles and sat on thrones. There was Babe Ruth, the Home-Run King of Baseball—he didn't wear a golden crown, but no king, who did, ever had so many devoted followers, especially among boys. After a game, boys crowded around him. Often one of them brought his own ball, with which he played on an empty lot near his home. He would ask Babe Ruth to autograph it. And the Babe, smiling his kindly smile, would always make the boy happy by autographing his ball.

But the mothers and fathers, the sisters and brothers of these boys, yes, even their grandpas and grandmas, idolized Babe Ruth, too! Everyone wanted to see him play. Never in the history of baseball had there been such a batter as he. He could hit a ball harder and more often, he could send it farther than any man who had ever lived. And he was winning game after game for the New York Yankees in the great battles of the World Series.

When the Yankee fans in the bleachers saw him come out of the dugout, pick up his bat and go loping off to the plate, they shouted for joy. He was a big man—that was why he was jokingly called "Babe." His real name was George Herman Ruth. As he raised his bat with his eye on the ball, the pitcher would throw that ball with all the skill he possessed to trick the Babe into missing it. But crack! He would hit it! He would send it flying so far that the men on other bases could all get in, "safe," and the Babe would make a home run.

Then the Yankee fans went wild. They roared, they jumped up and down, they threw their hats in the air. And over that part of the crowd who favored the opposing team there fell a terrible silence, a grim, dark cloud of gloom.

Babe Ruth broke all world records—he made sixty home-runs in one year. And during the twenty-two years that he played in big league baseball, he piled up 714 home-runs. No wonder people called him the Home-Run King!

But it was not for this reason only that people loved and admired Babe Ruth. They admired him because he always showed good sportsmanship. They admired him, too, because he had succeeded in spite of a difficult boyhood. And they loved him because he was always ready to help anyone in need and because he would take as much trouble to make a boy or girl happy as he would have taken to do a favor for the most important man in the country. Every boy wanted to be the kind of king that he was. Every boy wanted to be like Babe Ruth.

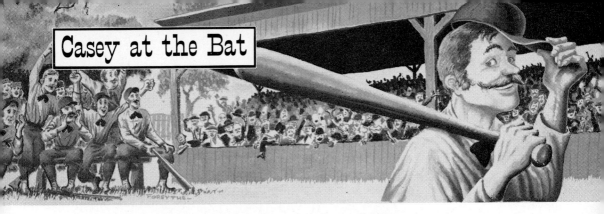

Casey at the Bat

A Tale of the Hero of Mudville

It looked extremely rocky for the Mudville nine that day;
The score stood two to four, with but an inning left to play.
So, when Cooney died at second, and Burrows did the same,
A pallor wreathed the features of the patrons of the game.

A straggling few got up to go, leaving there the rest,
With that hope which springs eternal within the human breast.
For they thought: "If only Casey could get a whack at that,"
They'd put even money now, with Casey at the bat.

But Flynn preceded Casey, and likewise so did Blake,
And the former was a "pudd'n," and the latter was a "fake."
So on that stricken multitude a deathlike silence sat;
For there seemed but little chance of Casey's getting to the bat.

But Flynn let drive a "single," to the wonderment of all.
And the much-despised Blakey "tore the cover off the ball."
And when the dust had lifted, and they saw what had occurred,
There was Blakey safe at second, and Flynn a-huggin' third.

Then from the gladdened multitude went up a joyous yell—
It rumbled in the mountaintops, it rattled in the dell;
It struck upon the hillside and rebounded on the flat;
For Casey, mighty Casey, was advancing to the bat.

There was ease in Casey's manner as he stepped into his place,
There was pride in Casey's bearing and a smile on Casey's face;
And when responding to the cheers he lightly doffed his hat,
No stranger in the crowd could doubt 'twas Casey at the bat.

Ten thousand eyes were on him as he rubbed his hands with dirt,
Five thousand tongues applauded when he wiped them on his shirt;
Then when the writhing pitcher ground the ball into his hip,
Defiance glanced in Casey's eye, a sneer curled Casey's lip.

And now the leather-covered sphere came hurtling through the air,
And Casey stood a-watching it in haughty grandeur there.
Close by the sturdy batsman the ball unheeded sped;
"That's not my style," said Casey. "Strike one," the umpire said.

From the benches, black with people, there went up a muffled roar,
Like the beating of the storm waves on the stern and distant shore.
"Kill him! Kill the umpire!" shouted someone on the stand;
And it's likely they'd have killed him had not Casey raised his hand.

With a smile of Christian charity great Casey's visage shone;
He stilled the rising tumult, he made the game go on;
He signaled to the pitcher, and once more the spheroid flew;
But Casey still ignored it, and the umpire said, "Strike two."

"Fraud!" cried the maddened thousands, and the echo answered,
        "Fraud!"
But one scornful look from Casey and the audience was awed;
They saw his face grow stern and cold, they saw his muscles strain,
And they knew that Casey wouldn't let the ball go by again.

The sneer is gone from Casey's lips, his teeth are clenched in hate,
He pounds with cruel vengeance his bat upon the plate;
And now the pitcher holds the ball, and now he lets it go,
And now the air is shattered by the force of Casey's blow.

Oh, somewhere in this favored land the sun is shining bright,
The band is playing somewhere, and somewhere hearts are light;
And somewhere men are laughing, and somewhere children shout,
But there is no joy in Mudville: Mighty Casey has struck out.

Ernest Lawrence Thayer

Casey's Comeback

A Reply to the Famous Baseball Classic, "CASEY AT THE BAT"

There were saddened hearts in Mudville for a week or even more;
There were muttered oaths and curses—every fan in town was "sore."
"Just think," said one, "how soft it looked with Casey at the bat!
And then to think he'd go and spring a bush-league trick like that."

All his past fame was forgotten; he was now a hopeless "shine,"
They called him "Strike-out Casey" from the mayor down the line,
And as he came to bat each day his bosom heaved a sigh,
While a look of hopeless fury shone in mighty Casey's eye.

The lane is long, someone has said, that never turns again,
And Fate, though fickle, often gives another chance to men.
And Casey smiled—his rugged face no longer wore a frown;
The pitcher who had started all the trouble came to town.

All Mudville had assembled; ten thousand fans had come
To see the twirler who had put big Casey "on the bum";
And when he stepped into the box the multitude went wild.
He doffed his cap in proud disdain—but Casey only smiled.

144f

"Play ball!" the umpire's voice rang out, and then the game began;
But in that throng of thousands there was not a single fan
Who thought that Mudville had a chance; and with the setting sun
Their hopes sank low—the rival team was leading "four to one."

The last half of the ninth came round, with no change in the score;
But when the first man up hit safe the crowd began to roar.
The din increased, the echo of ten thousand shouts was heard
When the pitcher hit the second and gave "four balls" to the third.

Three men on base—nobody out—three runs to tie the game!
A triple meant the highest niche in Mudville's hall of fame;
But here the rally ended and the gloom was deep as night
When the fourth one "fouled to catcher" and the fifth "flew out to
    right."

A dismal groan in chorus came—a scowl was on each face—
When Casey walked up, bat in hand, and slowly took his place;
His bloodshot eyes in fury gleamed; his teeth were clenched in hate;
He gave his cap a vicious hook and pounded on the plate.

But fame is fleeting as the wind, and glory fades away;
There were no wild and woolly cheers, no glad acclaim this day.
They hissed and groaned and hooted as they clamored, "Strike him
    out!"
But Casey gave no outward sign that he had heard this shout.

The pitcher smiled and cut one loose; across the plate it spread;
Another hiss, another groan. "Strike one!" the umpire said.
Zip! Like a shot, the second curve broke just below his knee—
"Strike two!" the umpire roared aloud; but Casey made no plea.

No roasting for the umpire now—his was an easy lot;
But here the pitcher whirled again—was that a rifle shot?
A whack! a crack! and out through space the leather pellet flew,
A blot against the distant sky, a speck against the blue.

Above the fence in center field, in rapid whirling flight,
The sphere sailed on; the blot grew dim and then was lost to sight.
Ten thousand hats were thrown in air, ten thousand threw a fit;
But no one ever found the ball that mighty Casey hit!

Oh, somewhere in this favored land dark clouds may hide the sun,
And somewhere bands no longer play and children have no fun;
And somewhere over blighted lives there hangs a heavy pall;
But Mudville hearts are happy now—for Casey hit the ball!

James Wilson

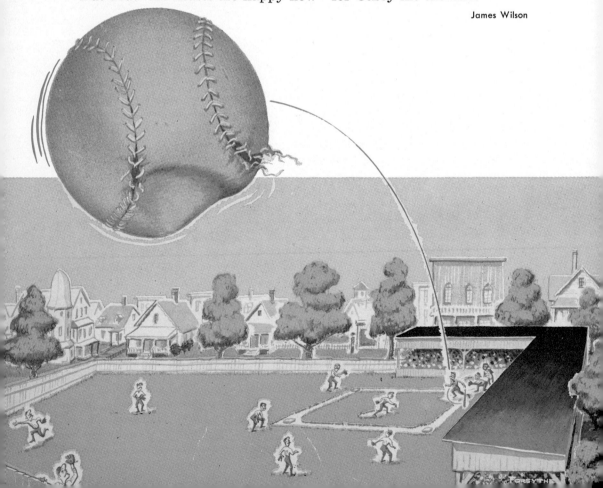

THE PEDDLER'S SONG*
WILLIAM SHAKESPEARE

WILL you buy any tape,
  Or lace for your cape,
My dainty duck, my dear-O?
  Any silk, any thread,
  Any toys for your head
Of the newest and finest, finest wear-O?

Lawn as white as driven snow,
  Crepe as black as e'er was crow,
Gloves as sweet as damask roses
  Masks for faces and for noses,
Bugle bracelet, necklace amber,
  Perfume for a lady's chamber,
Golden quoifs and stomachers,
  For my lads to give their dears,
Pins and poking sticks of steel
  What maids lack from head to heel,
Come buy of me! Come! Come buy! Come buy!
  Buy, lads, or else your lasses cry!
    Come buy!

*From *A Winter's Tale*, Act IV, Scene iv. See the story of *A Winter's Tale* beginning on page 144.

The Winter's Tale

*From Tales from Shakespeare**

CHARLES AND MARY LAMB

LEONTES, king of Sicily, and his queen, the beautiful and virtuous Hermione, once lived in the greatest harmony together. So happy was Leontes in the love of this excellent lady, that he had no wish ungratified, except that he sometimes desired to see again and to present to his queen his old companion and schoolfellow, Polixenes, king of Bohemia. Leontes and Polixenes were brought up together from their infancy, but, being by the death of their fathers called to reign over their respective kingdoms, they had not met for many years, though they frequently interchanged gifts, letters, and loving embassies.

At length, after repeated invitations, Polixenes came from Bohemia to the Sicilian court to make his friend Leontes a visit.

At first this visit gave nothing but pleasure to Leontes. He recommended the friend of his youth to the queen's particular attention and seemed, in the presence of his dear friend and old companion, to have his felicity quite completed. They talked over old times. Their schooldays and their youthful pranks were remembered and recounted to Hermione, who always took a cheerful part in these conversations.

When, after a long stay, Polixenes was preparing to depart, Hermione, at the desire of her husband, joined her entreaties to his that Polixenes would prolong his visit.

And now began this good queen's sorrow, for Polixenes, refusing to stay at the request of Leontes, was won over by Hermione's gentle and persuasive words to put off his departure for some weeks longer. Upon this, although Leontes had so long known the integrity and honourable principles of his friend Polixenes as well as the excellent disposition of his virtuous queen, he was seized with an ungovernable jealousy.

Tales from Shakespeare by the brother and sister, Charles and Mary Lamb, were written in 1807.

THE MAGIC GARDEN

Every attention Hermione showed to Polixenes, though by her husband's particular desire and merely to please him, increased the unfortunate king's jealousy; and, from being a loving and a true friend and the best and fondest of husbands, Leontes became suddenly a savage and inhuman monster. Sending for Camillo, one of the lords of his court, and telling him of the suspicion he entertained, he commanded him to poison Polixenes.

Camillo was a good man; and he, well-knowing that the jealousy of Leontes had not the slightest foundation in truth, instead of poisoning Polixenes acquainted him with the king's orders, and agreed to escape with him out of the Sicilian dominions. Polixenes, with the assistance of Camillo, arrived safe in his own kingdom of Bohemia, where Camillo lived from that time in the king's court and became the chief friend and favourite of Polixenes.

The flight of Polixenes enraged the jealous Leontes still more. He went to the queen's apartment where the good lady was sitting with her little son Mamillus, who was just beginning to tell one of his best stories to amuse his mother, when the king entered and taking the child away, sent Hermione to prison. Mamillus, though but a very young child, loved his mother tenderly, and, when he saw her so dishonoured and found she was taken from him to be put into prison, took it deeply to heart and drooped and pined away by slow degrees, losing his appetite and his sleep, till it was thought his grief would kill him.

The king, when he had sent his queen to prison, commanded Cleomenes and Dion, two Sicilian lords, to go to Delphos, there to inquire of the oracle at the temple of Apollo if his queen had been unfaithful.

147

When Hermione had been a short time in prison, she was brought to bed of a daughter, and the poor lady received much comfort from the sight of her pretty baby. She said to it, "My poor little prisoner, I am as innocent as you are."

Hermione had a kind friend in the noble-spirited Paulina, who was the wife of Antigonus, a Sicilian lord; and, when the lady Paulina heard her royal mistress was brought to bed, she went to the prison where Hermione was confined. She said to Emilia, a lady who attended upon Hermione, "I pray you, Emilia, tell the good queen if her majesty dare trust me with her little babe, I will carry it to the king, its father. We do not know how he may soften at the sight of his innocent child."

"Most worthy madam," replied Emilia, "I will acquaint the queen with your noble offer. She was wishing today that she had any friend who would venture to present the child to the king."

"And tell her," said Paulina, "that I will speak boldly to Leontes in her defence."

"May you be forever blessed," said Emilia, "for your kindness to our gracious queen!" Emilia then went to Hermione, who joyfully gave up her baby to the care of Paulina, for she had feared that no one would dare venture to present the child to its father. Paulina took the new-born infant and forcing herself into the king's presence, notwithstanding her husband, fearing the king's anger, endeavoured to prevent her, she laid the babe at its father's feet. Paulina made a noble speech to the king in defence of Hermione;

and she reproached him severely for his inhumanity and implored him to have mercy on his innocent wife and child. But Paulina's spirited remonstrances only aggravated Leontes' displeasure, and he ordered her husband, Antigonus, to take her from his presence. When Paulina went away, she left the little baby at its father's feet, thinking when he was alone with it, he would look upon it and have pity on its helpless innocence.

The good Paulina was mistaken; for no sooner was she gone than the merciless father ordered Antigonus, Paulina's husband, to take the child and carry it out to sea and leave it upon some desert shore to perish. Antigonus, unlike the good Camillo, too well obeyed the orders of Leontes. He immediately carried the child on shipboard and put out to sea, intending to leave it on the first desert coast he could find.

So firmly was the king persuaded of the guilt of Hermione that he would not wait for the return of Cleomenes and Dion, whom he had sent to consult the oracle of Apollo at Delphos. But, before the queen was recovered from her lying-in and from her grief for the loss of her precious baby, he had her brought to a public trial before all the lords and nobles of his court.

When all the great lords, the judges, and all the nobility of the land were assembled together to try Hermione, and that unhappy queen was standing as a prisoner before her subjects to receive their judgment, Cleomenes and Dion entered the assembly and presented to the king the answer of the oracle, sealed up. Leontes commanded the seal to be broken and the words of the oracle to be read aloud. These were the words:—"Hermione is innocent, Polixenes blameless, Camillo a true subject, Leontes a jealous tyrant, and the king shall live without an heir if that which is lost be not found." The king would give no credit to the words of the oracle. He said it was falsehood invented by the queen's friends, and he desired the judge to proceed with the trial. But while Leontes was speaking, a man entered and told him that the Prince Mamillus, hearing his mother was to be tried for her life, had suddenly died. Hermione, upon hearing of the death of this dear, affectionate child, fainted; and Leontes, pierced to the heart by the news, began to feel pity for his unhappy queen. He ordered Paulina and the ladies who were her attendants, to take her away and use means for her recovery. Paulina soon returned and told the king that Hermione was dead.

When Leontes heard that the queen was dead, he repented of his cruelty to her; and now that he thought his ill-usage had broken Hermione's heart, he believed her innocent. Now he thought the words of the oracle were true, as he knew "if that which was lost was not found," which he concluded was his young daughter, he should be without an heir, the young Prince Mamillus being dead. He would now give his kingdom to recover his lost daughter: and Leontes gave himself up to remorse, and passed many years in mournful thoughts and repentant grief.

The ship in which Antigonus carried the infant princess out to sea was driven by a storm upon the coast of Bohemia, the very kingdom of the good King Polixenes. Here Antigonus landed and here he left the little baby.

THE MAGIC GARDEN

Antigonus never returned to Sicily to tell Loentes where he had left his daughter, for, as he was going back to the ship, a bear came out of the woods and tore him to pieces; a just punishment on him for obeying the wicked order of Leontes.

The child was dressed in rich clothes and jewels; for Hermione had made it very fine when she sent it to Leontes, and Antigonus had pinned a paper to its mantle with the name of Perdita written thereon—words obscurely intimating her high birth and untoward fate. This poor deserted baby was found by a shepherd. He was a humane man, and so he carried the little Perdita home to his wife, who nursed her tenderly. But poverty tempted the shepherd to conceal the rich prize he had found. Therefore, he left that part of the country, that no one might know where he got his riches; and, with part of Perdita's jewels, he bought herds of sheep and became a wealthy shepherd. He brought up Perdita as his own child, and she knew not she was any other than a shepherd's daughter.

The little Perdita grew up a lovely maiden. Though she had no better education than that of a shepherd's daughter, yet so did the natural graces she inherited from her royal mother shine forth in her untutored mind, that no one from her behavior would have known she had not been brought up in her father's court.

Polixenes, the king of Bohemia, had an only son, whose name was Florizel. As this young prince was hunting near the shepherd's dwelling, he saw the old man's supposed daughter; and the beauty, modesty, and queen-like deportment of Perdita caused him to fall instantly in love with her. He soon, under the name of Doricles and in the disguise of a private gentleman, became a constant visitor at the old shepherd's house.

Florizel's frequent absences from court alarmed Polixenes. Setting people to watch his son, he discovered his love for the shepherd's fair daughter. Polixenes then called for Camillo, the faithful Camillo who had preserved his life from the fury of

Leontes, and he desired that Camillo would accompany him to the house of the shepherd, who was the supposed father of Perdita.

Polixenes and Camillo, both in disguise, arrived at the old shepherd's dwelling while they were celebrating the feast of sheep-shearing. And, though they were strangers, yet at the sheep-shearing every guest being made welcome, they were invited to come in and join in the general festivity. Nothing but mirth and jollity was going forward. Tables were spread and great preparations were making for the rustic feast. Some lads and lasses were dancing on the green before the house, while others of the young men were buying ribands, gloves, and such toys of a peddler.

CORINA MELDER-COLLIER

THE MAGIC GARDEN

While this busy scene was going forward, Florizel and Perdita sat quietly in a retired corner, seemingly more pleased with the conversation of each other than desirous of engaging in the sports of those around them. The king was so disguised that it was impossible his son could know him. He, therefore, advanced near enough to hear the conversation. The simple yet elegant manner in which Perdita conversed with his son did not a little surprise Polixenes. He said to Camillo, "This is the prettiest low-born lass I ever saw. Nothing she does or says but looks like something greater than herself, too noble for this place."

Camillo replied, "Indeed, she is the *queen* of curds and cream."

"Pray, my good friend," said the king to the old shepherd, "what fair swain is that talking with your daughter?"

"They call him Doricles," replied the shepherd. "He says he loves my daughter; and, to speak truth, there is not a kiss to choose which loves the other best. If young Doricles can get her, she shall bring him that he little dreams of," meaning the remainder of Perdita's jewels, which, after he had bought herds of sheep, he had carefully hoarded up for her marriage portion.

Polixenes then addressed his son. "How now, young man!"

153

said he, "your heart seems full of something that takes off your mind from feasting. When I was young, I used to load my love with presents; but you have let the peddler go and have bought your lass no toy."

The young prince, who little thought he was talking to his father, replied: "Old sir, she prizes not such trifles; the gifts which Perdita expects from me are locked up in my heart." Then turning to Perdita, he said, "O hear me, Perdita, before this ancient gentleman, who it seems was once himself a lover; he shall hear what I profess." Florizel then called upon the old stranger to be a witness to a solemn promise of marriage which he made to Perdita, saying to Polixenes, "I pray you, mark our contract."

"Mark your divorce, young sir," said the king, discovering himself. Polixenes then reproached his son for daring to contract himself to this low-born maiden, calling Perdita "shepherd's-brat," "sheep-hook," and other disrespectful names, and threatening if ever she suffered his son to see her again, he would put her and the old shepherd, her father, to a cruel death.

The king then left them in great wrath and ordered Camillo to follow him with Prince Florizel. When the king had departed, Perdita, whose royal nature was roused by Polixenes' reproaches, said: "Though we are all undone, I was not much afraid. Once or twice I was about to speak and tell him plainly that the selfsame sun which shines upon his palace hides not his face from our cottage, but looks on both alike." Then sorrowfully she said, "But now I am awakened from this dream, I will queen it no further. Leave me, sir; I will go milk my ewes and weep."

The kind-hearted Camillo was charged with the spirit and propriety of Perdita's behavior; and, perceiving that the young prince was too deeply in love to give up his mistress at the command of his father, he thought of a way to befriend the lovers and, at the same time, execute a favourite scheme he had in mind.

Camillo had long known that Leontes, the king of Sicily, was become a true penitent; and, though Camillo was now the favoured friend of King Polixenes, he could not help wishing once more to see his late royal master and his native home. He therefore proposed to Florizel and Perdita, that they should accompany him to the Sicilian court where he would engage Leontes should protect them, till, through his mediation, they could obtain pardon from Polixenes and his consent to their marriage.

To this proposal, they joyfully agreed. Camillo, who conducted everything relative to their flight, allowed the old shepherd to go along with them. The shepherd took with him the remainder of Perdita's jewels, her baby clothes, and the paper which he had found pinned to her mantle.

After a prosperous voyage, Florizel and Perdita, Camillo and the old shepherd arrived in safety at the court of Leontes. Leontes, who still mourned his dead Hermione and his lost child, received Camillo with great kindness and gave a cordial welcome to Prince Florizel. But Perdita, whom Florizel introduced as his princess, seemed to engross all Leontes' attention. Perceiving a resemblance between her and his dead queen, Hermione, his grief broke out afresh and he said such a lovely creature might his own daughter have been, if he had not so cruelly destroyed her. "Then, too," said he to Florizel, "I lost the society and friendship of your brave father, whom I now desire more than life once again to look upon."

When the old shepherd heard how much notice the king had taken of Perdita and that he had lost a daughter, who was exposed in infancy, he fell to comparing the time when he found Perdita with the manner of her exposure, the jewels, and other tokens of her high birth; from all which it was impossible for him not to conclude that Perdita and the king's lost daughter were the same.

Florizel and Perdita, Camillo and the faithful Paulina were present when the old shepherd related to the king the manner in which he had found the child, and also the circumstances of Antigonus' death, he having seen the bear seize upon him.

He showed the rich mantle in which Paulina remembered Hermione had wrapped the child, he produced a jewel which she remembered Hermione had tied about Perdita's neck, and he gave up the paper which Paulina knew to be the writing of her husband. It could not be doubted that Perdita was Leontes' own daughter; but oh, the noble struggles of Paulina between sorrow for her husband's death and joy that the oracle was fulfilled, in that the king's heir, his long-lost daughter was found.

When Leontes heard that Perdita was his daughter, the great sorrow that he felt that Hermione was not living to behold her child made him so sad that he could say nothing for a long time but, "O thy mother, thy mother!"

Paulina interrupted this joyful yet distressful scene, with saying to Leontes that she had a statue newly finished by that rare Italian master, Julio Romano, which was such a perfect resemblance of the queen, that would his majesty be pleased to go to her house and look upon it, he would be almost ready to think it was Hermione herself. Thither they then all went. The king anxious to see the semblance of his Hermione, and Perdita longing to behold what the mother, she never saw, did look like.

When Paulina drew back the curtain which concealed this famous statue, so perfectly did it resemble Hermione that all the king's sorrow was renewed at the sight. For a long time, he had no power to speak or move.

"I like your silence, my liege," said Paulina, "it the more shows your wonder. Is not this statue very like your queen?"

At length the king said, "O thus she stood, even with such majesty, when I first wooed her. But yet, Paulina, Hermione was not so aged as this statue looks."

Paulina replied, "So much the more the carver's excellence, who has made the statue as Hermione would have looked had she been living now. But let me draw the curtain, Sire, lest presently you think it moves."

THE MAGIC GARDEN

The king then said, "Do not draw the curtain! Would I were dead! See, Camillo, would you not think it breathed? Her eye seems to have motion in it. Would you not think her alive?"

"I must draw the curtain, my liege," said Paulina. "You are so transported, you will persuade yourself the statue lives."

"O Paulina," said Leontes, "make me think so twenty years! Methinks there is an air comes from her. What fine chisel could ever yet cut breath? Let no man mock me, for I will kiss her."

"Good, my lord, forbear!" said Paulina. "The ruddiness upon her lip is wet; you will stain your own with oily painting. Shall I draw the curtain?"

"No, not these twenty years," said Leontes.

Perdita, who all this time had been kneeling and beholding in silent admiration the statue of her matchless mother, now said, "And so long could I stay here, looking upon my dear mother."

"Either forbear this transport," said Paulina to Leontes, "and let me draw the curtain, or prepare yourself for more amazement. I can make the statue move indeed, ay, and descend from

the pedestal and take you by the hand. But then you will think, which I protest I am not, that I am assisted by some wicked powers."

"What you can, make her do!" said the astonished king. "I am content to look upon. What you can, make her speak! I am content to hear, for it is as easy to make her speak as move."

Paulina then ordered some slow and solemn music, which she had prepared for the purpose, and, to the amazement of all the beholders, the statue came down from the pedestal and threw its arms around Leontes' neck. The statue then began to speak, praying for blessings on her husband and her child, the newly-found Perdita.

THE MAGIC GARDEN

No wonder that the statue hung upon Leontes' neck, and blessed her husband and her child. No wonder! For the statue was indeed Hermione herself—the real, the living queen!

Paulina had falsely reported to the king the death of Hermione, thinking that the only means to preserve her royal mistress' life; and with the good Paulina, Hermione had lived ever since, never choosing Leontes should know she was living till she heard Perdita was found. For, though she had long forgiven the injuries which Leontes had done to her, she could not pardon his cruelty to his infant daughter. His dead queen thus restored to life, his lost daughter found, the long-sorrowing Leontes could scarcely support the excess of his own happiness.

Nothing but congratulations and affectionate speeches were heard on all sides. Now the delighted parent thanked Prince Florizel for loving their lowly-seeming daughter; and now they blessed the good old shepherd for preserving their child. Greatly did Camillo and Paulina rejoice that they had lived to see so good an end of all their faithful services.

And, as if nothing should be wanting to complete this strange and unlooked-for joy, King Polixenes himself now entered the palace. When Polixenes first missed his son and Camillo, knowing that Camillo had long wished to return to Sicily, he conjectured he should find the fugitives here; and, following them with all speed, he happened to arrive just at this, the happiest moment of Leontes' life.

Polixenes took part in the general joy. He forgave his friend Leontes the unjust jealousy he had conceived against him, and they once more loved each other with all the warmth of their first boyish friendship. And there was no fear that Polixenes would now oppose his son's marriage with Perdita.

Thus have we seen the patient virtues of the long-suffering Hermione rewarded. That excellent lady lived many years with Leontes and Perdita, the happiest of mothers and of queens.

The Renowned and World-Famous
Adventures of Punch and Judy

"SQUEAK! Sque-eak!" Here's old Mr. Punch again, popping out from the curtains to welcome the crowd before him. Old Mr. Punch with his great hooked nose and his hooked chin and his peaked cap. And he has with him his wife, Judy, and the baby who is always being thrown out the window, and Toby, the dog, and the hobby horse and all the rest of the well-known, widely-travelled, world-famous performers in the puppet show! And old Mr. Punch says:

> *"Ladies and gentlemen, pray how you do?*★
> *If you all happy, me all happy too.*
> *Stop and hear my merry little play,*
> *If me make you laugh, me need not*
> ***make** you pay!"*

There's hardly a corner of the world Punch and Judy haven't visited, and they've been sending men, women, and children into gales of laughter from Boston to Paris, from China to Peru, for nobody knows how many hundreds of years. So you see Punch and Judy are people of renown.

A hundred years ago in any great city of Europe or America, one might have seen set up in some public place, a little movable box of a theatre in which all the actors were wooden dolls — puppets or marionettes, as they are called. Sometimes these puppets were made to move about and go through the action of the play by means of wires attached to their heads; sometimes the man who gave the show stood inside a box below the little stage and wore Punch and Judy on his hands, which were covered from sight by the clothes of the puppets. He would use his thumb and middle finger to move the arms and his forefinger for the head. Then Mr. Punch, and Mrs. Judy, and the baby,

★Since many puppet showmen were Italians, the English they used in making the characters talk was often nearly as strange as that of the distinguished foreign gentleman! Each showman made up his own words for the characters to speak but the actual story of the play has been little changed from the beginning.

and the hobby horse, and the distinguished foreign gentleman who couldn't speak English, and the rest would go through their parts with much spirit, while the showman made up the words they were supposed to speak to each other, as the play went on.

Some of the puppet shows in London remained always in one place and were so loved by the people that real actors and singers, at the opera, complained because their play houses were empty while everybody crowded to see the puppet shows. There was even one droll showman who trained a little pig to dance with Mr. Punch and squeak as if he were singing in imitation of one of the great Italian opera singers of the day.

Other puppet shows, instead of remaining always in one place, were carried about, both in town and in the country, on the backs of strolling showmen. These were particularly popular at country fairs, where they drew great crowds of merry, laughter-loving people. One man would carry the theatre itself on his back, and the other the box in which the puppets were packed. The first man would blow a little tin whistle and the second a trumpet to attract people's attention and, wherever they found a crowd gathered together or saw signs of interest, they set up their theatre and gave a performance. As soon as

Mr. Punch showed his ridiculous hooked nose between the curtains and gave the squeak that always announces his appearances,
the people began to laugh, and they never left off laughing till
the show was over. One of the men would pass about among
the on-lookers and collect pennies during the play, and then off
they would go to find another crowd.

The puppet shows came to England from Italy, but long,
long, before that time, in the year 1000 B. C. or thereabouts, it
is said that a puppet showman gave a performance before the
Emperor of China. That august gentleman had never heard of
a puppet show and he thought that the dolls must be live men
who dared to make faces at him. At last, becoming angry at
their grimaces, he ordered all their heads off! The showman
with great difficulty was able to persuade the Emperor that the
actors were only dolls, whereupon, not only did he escape punishment, but was rewarded for his cleverness by being made
official puppet showman of the Chinese Empire.

Since Mr. Punch first appeared in the world the story about
him has been little changed, although it was part of the showman's business to make up new lines for the characters to speak
as the play went on. Mr. Punch has been from the beginning
and still is, the most ridiculous, absurd, impossible old rascal
and villain in the world! He beats his wife, lays everybody else
out with his stick, and flings his baby out the window quite
unconcerned about it all, ever smiling, ever dancing and singing,
without a pang of sorrow or regret. In the end he comes off
victorious and conquers all his enemies without ever once being
punished for his sins!

Once a very serious-minded showman was so disturbed at
Punch's always coming off victorious in spite of his evil deeds,
that he made bold to change the ending of the play, and have
Punch meet his just punishment, but the crowd round about

wouldn't have it—not at all. They pelted the poor man and his show with mud and drove him away.

So here is the Punch and Judy show as it has been given with slight variations for hundreds of years.

As the curtains are drawn back Mr. Punch is heard singing down below the stage,

> *"I dreamt that I dwelt in marble halls*
> *With vassals and serfs by my si-hi-hide!"*

All of a sudden up he pops like a jack-in-the-box, shouting for his wife—"Judy, Judy, Judy!"

Instead of Judy, in comes the little dog Toby.

"Hello, Toby!" says Punch. "Who called you? How do you do, Mr. Toby? Hope you very well, Mr. Toby."

"Bow, wow, wow!" says Toby.

"I'm glad to hear it, Toby! What a nice, good dog you are! Good Toby! Good Toby!"

At that Toby snarls, "Arr-rr! Arr-rr!"

"What, Toby, you cross this morning? You get out of bed the wrong way upwards?"

"Arr-rr! Arr-rr," answers Toby.

Punch puts out his hand cautiously to coax the dog. "Good doggie! Good doggie! Be a good doggie and me give you some pail of water and a broomstick for supper!"

But Toby snaps at his hand. Then Punch grows very angry and yells:

"Toby, you're one bad dog! Get away with you!" And he strikes at the dog with his stick. Just at that moment Mr. Scaramouch, the owner of the dog, rises from below the stage and Bang! he gets square on his head the blow Mr. Punch had intended for Toby.

"Ow-wow!" squeals Mr. Scaramouch, "I shall make you pay for my head, sir!"

"And I shall make you pay for my stick, sir!"

"I haven't broken your stick!"

"And I haven't broken your head!"

"You have, sir!"

"Then it must have been cracked before!"

"Hello," cries Mr. Scaramouch, spying Toby, "why, that's my dog Toby. Toby, old fellow, how are you?" Toby barks.

"He isn't your dog!" cries Punch.

"He is!"

"He isn't!"

"He is, I tell you! A fortnight ago I lost him."

"And a fortnight ago I found him!"

"We'll soon see whether he belongs to you!" shouts Mr. Scaramouch. "You shall go up to him and say, 'Toby, poor little fellow, how are you?' "

"Very good!" agrees Mr. Punch, and he goes up to Toby, saying, "Toby, poor little fellow, how are you?" Toby snaps at Punch's nose.

"There you see that shows the dog is mine!" yells Scaramouch.

"No!" cries Punch, "it shows he's mine!"

"If he's yours, why does he bite you?"

"He bites me because he likes me!"

"Nonsense!" cries Scaramouch. "We'll soon settle which of us the dog belongs to. We'll fight for him. Now don't you begin till I say 'Time!' "

Punch knocks Mr. Scaramouch down and Scaramouch howls, "That wasn't fair!"

"It was fair!" cries Punch, "I didn't hit till you cried 'Time'."

"I never did!" goes on Mr. Scaramouch. "I only said, 'Don't begin till I say 'Time.' " Punch knocks him down a second time. "There you said it again!"

Scaramouch roars, "Toby, come help your master." The dog springs forward. Seeing this Punch begins to squeal, "No, no! Call off the dog! It isn't fair! You didn't say 'Time!'" Toby barks furiously and seizes Punch by the nose.

"Oh dear! Oh dear!" squeaks Punch, "My nose! My poor nose! My pretty little nose! My beautiful nose!" He tries to shake off the dog, but Toby still clings to his nose as he dances wildly around the stage. "Murder! Fire! Thieves! Call off your dog!"

"Very well," says Mr. Scaramouch, "come along, Toby!"

Toby lets go and the two leave the stage.

"I wouldn't have that dog as a gift," says Punch, nursing his nose and calling once again for Judy.

Judy comes in, in a frilled cap, with a hooked nose and hooked chin, just as ugly as Mr. Punch. "Well, what do you want now I've come?" says she.

165

"Ah," says Punch in a wheedling tone, "what a pretty little creature! Ain't she one beauty? Why, I want to dance with you, my duckie!" They dance. At the conclusion of the dance Punch hits Judy over the head with his stick.

"You villain," cries Judy, "how dare you strike me? Take that!" and she slaps him in the face.

"Ah," says Punch, stroking his cheek, "she is always so playful! Bring me the child, Judy! Bring me the child!"

Judy goes and brings back the baby which she leaves with Punch. He dandles the child in his arms and sings:

"Dancy baby diddy;
What shall daddy do widdy?
Sit on his lap,
Give it some pap;
Dancy, baby, diddy."

"What a pretty baby it is," he croons, "little duck! Never was such a good child!"

The Baby cries, "Mama-a-a-a!"

Punch thumps the child with his stick.

"Go to sleep, my pretty!" he cries.

Baby cries louder, "Mama-a-a-a!"

Punch whacks him harder still, singing, "Hush-a-bye! Hush! Hush! Hush-sh-sh!"

Baby yells "Ya-a-ah!" and catches hold of Punch's nose.

"Murder! Let go!" howls Punch. "Go to your mother, darling,"—and Biff! he throws the baby out the window. Then he sings, smiling and unconcerned:

"I dreamt that I dwelt in marble halls,
With vassals and serfs by my si-hi-hide!"

At that, in comes Judy.

"Where's the boy?" she cries.

"Why, didn't you catch him?" asks Punch.

"Catch him?" says Judy. "What have you done with him?"

"Oh," cries Punch, "I just threw him out the window! Thought you might be passing and catch him."

"Oh you horrid wretch!" shrieks Judy. "You shall pay for this!" She hurries out, comes back in a moment with a stick, and hits Punch a resounding blow on the head, continuing then to pound him. "I'll teach you to drop my child out the window!"

"Ow-wow," howls Punch. "I'll never do it again!"

"I'll teach you! I'll teach you!"

"Then I be teacher too!" cries Punch. He takes the stick from Judy and knocks her flat with a blow, then he goes on singing:
*"I dreamt that I dwelt in marble halls,
    With vassals and serfs by my si-hi-hide."*

In comes a policeman brandishing his club.

"Hollo! Hollo! Hollo! Here I am!" cries the policeman.

"Hollo! Hollo! Hollo!" answers Punch. "Here I am too!" and he whacks the policeman over the head!

"Do you see my club, sir?" shouts the policeman.

"Do you feel my stick, sir?" answers Punch.

"Take your nose out of my face, sir!"

"Take your face out of my nose, sir!"

"Pooh!" cries the policeman.

"Pooh!" answers Punch.

"You have committed a crime, sir," says the policeman, "and I am come to take you up."

"And I am come to knock you down!" retorts Punch. Whack! He lays the policeman flat and goes on singing and dancing as before. Then he gets a great sheep bell and begins to shake it all about the stage. There enters a foreign servant dressed in outlandish livery.

"Mr. Punch," says the servant, "my master he say he no lika de noise."

Punch mimics him, "Your master he say he no lika de noise! What noise?"

"Dat horrid, bad noise! He'll no have more noise near his house!"

"He won't, won't he?" And Punch runs about the stage shaking the bell as loudly as before.

"Get away I say wid dat horrid, bad bell," says the servant.

"Do you call that a bell," says Punch, "it's an organ!"

"I say it is a bell, a horrid bad bell!"

"I say it is an organ!" And Punch pounds him with it. "What you say it is now?"

"Ow-wow! Stop! Stop! It is an organ!" cries the servant.

"An organ? I say it is a fiddle!" Punch offers to pound him again.

"It is a fiddle," agrees the servant.

"I say it is a drum," yells Punch.

"It is a drum," agrees the servant.

"I say it is a trumpet," yells Punch.

"Well, so it is a trumpet; but bell, organ, fiddle, drum or trumpet, my master he no lika de music."

"Not like my sweet music?" says Punch. "I'll teach you to like sweet music!" And he pounds the servant about the stage with the bell till he runs away. Then comes in the distinguished foreign gentleman himself, who, being unable to express himself in English, says very solemnly,

"Shallaballah!"

"Why don't you speak English?" asks Punch.

"Shallaballah!" answers the foreign gentleman.

"Then I'll hit you with my stick," says Punch.

"Shallaballah!" says the foreign gentleman.

Punch hits him over the head and he falls to the ground. Then Punch sings as before:

"I dreamt that I dwelt in marble halls
With vassals and serfs by my si-hi-hide!"

THE MAGIC GARDEN

Suddenly the image of all Mr. Punch's evil deeds in the form of a ghost peeps around a corner of the stage and whispers,

"Booh!" then disappears again.

Punch throws up his arms in alarm and says, "Ah, ah! I didn't do anything! It wasn't me!"

At that, all the people whom Punch has laid out on the stage rise straight up in the air, point their fingers accusingly at him, and, float away.

"Oh dear! Oh dear!" cries Punch. "A horse! My Kingdom for a horse!" Suddenly his hobby horse comes prancing in. Punch tries to mount him in order to run away but the horse rears up and throws him.

"Oh dear! Oh dear!" moans Punch, from the ground and then in comes the Hangman. The Hangman says:

"Mr. Punch, you are my prisoner! You have broken the laws of your country!"

"Broken the laws?" whines Punch picking himself up. "I couldn't break 'em. I never touched 'em!"

"I have come to hang you!" says the Hangman.

"Oh dear! Oh dear! Spare me! I've a wife and sixteen small children! What will they do without me?"

Nevertheless the Hangman produces a rope with a noose at the end, and this he throws over the limb of a tree.

"Come here!" says he.

"I can't," wails Punch. "I've a bone in my leg!"

"Then I must fetch you!" The two struggle and the Hangman takes Punch over to the tree.

"Put your head in here," says the Hangman, showing the noose.

"I don't know how! Show me!" whines Punch.

"Why it's easy! Just like this," says the Hangman. He puts his own head in the noose to show Punch how. Punch quickly pulls the rope and strings up the Hangman. "Oee! Oee!" he squeaks and begins to sing again. At that the ghost rises slowly.

"You are come for," he says in a hollow voice.

"Oh dear! Oh dear! What for?" cries Punch.

"To be carried off for your evil deeds, to the land of Bobbety Shooty."

The ghost approaches, still repeating in his hollow voice, "To be carried off for your evil deeds, to be carried off. To be carried off."

"That for my evil deeds," cries Punch. He hits the ghost himself on the head and biff! that's the end of the ghost. Then he jumps on his hobby horse and rides away, singing:

"Right tol de rol, it serves him right,
Now all my foes are put to flight,
Ladies and gentlemen all, good night,
To the freaks of Punch and Judy!"

SONG ON MAY MORNING

John Milton

NOW the bright morning star, Day's harbinger,
    Comes dancing from the East, and leads with her
The flowery May, who from her green lap throws
The yellow cowslip and the pale primrose.
Hail, bounteous May, that doth inspire
Mirth, and youth, and warm desire;
Woods and groves are of thy dressing,
Hill and dale doth boast thy blessing.
Thus we salute thee with our early song,
And welcome thee, and wish thee long.

Many English songs and dances celebrate May. The dance *Green Sleeves*, popular in Elizabethan days, is still danced in England. The modern composer, Percy Grainger, has used English folk music for the theme of *Shepherd's Hey, Country Gardens, Molly on the Shore.*

THE RAGGLE, TAGGLE GYPSIES

'Twas late last night when my lord came home,
  Inquiring for his lady, O.
The servants said on every hand,
  "She's gone with the Raggle, Taggle Gypsies, O."

Oh, he rode high and he rode low,
  He rode through woods and copses, O,
Until he came to an open field,
  And there he espied his lady, O.

"What makes you leave your house and lands?
  What makes you leave your money, O?
What makes you leave your new-wedded lord
  To go with the Raggle, Taggle Gypsies, O?"

"What care I for my house and lands?
  What care I for my money, O,
What care I for my new-wedded lord?
  I'm off with the Raggle, Taggle Gypsies, O."
                    —*Old Folk Song*

THE MAGIC GARDEN

The Knights of the Silver Shield*

Raymond MacDonald Alden

THERE was once a splendid castle in a forest, with great stone walls and a high gateway, and turrets that rose away above the tallest trees. The forest was dark and dangerous, and many cruel giants lived in it; but in the castle was a company of knights, who were kept there by the king of the country, to help travelers who might be in the forest, and to fight with the giants.

Each of these knights wore a beautiful suit of armor and carried a long spear, while over his helmet there floated a great red plume that could be seen a long way off by any one in distress. But the most wonderful thing about the knights' armor was their shields. They were not like those of other knights, but had been made by a great magician who had lived in the castle many years before. They were made of silver, and sometimes shone in the sunlight with dazzling brightness; but at other times the surface of the shields would be clouded as though by a mist, and one could not see his face reflected there.

*From *Why the Chimes Ring.* Copyright used by special permission of the Bobbs-Merrill Co.

173

Now, when each young knight received his spurs and his armor, a new shield was also given him from among those that the magician had made; and when the shield was new its surface was always cloudy and dull. But as the knight began to do service against the giants, or went on expeditions to help poor travelers in the forest, his shield grew brighter and brighter, so that he could see his face clearly reflected in it. But if he proved to be a lazy or cowardly knight, and let the giants get the better of him, or did not care what became of the travelers, then the shield grew more and more cloudy, until the knight became ashamed to carry it.

But this was not all. When any one of the knights fought a particularly hard battle, and won the victory, or when he went on some hard errand for the lord of the castle, and was successful, not only did his silver shield grow brighter, but when one looked into the center of it he could see something like a golden star shining in its very heart. This was the greatest honor that a knight could achieve, and the other knights always spoke of such a one as having "won his star." It was usually not till he was pretty old and tried as a soldier that he could win it. At the time when this story begins, the lord of the castle himself was the only one of the knights whose shield bore the golden star.

There came a time when the worst of the giants in the forest gathered themselves together to have a battle against the knights. They made a camp in a dark hollow not far from the castle, and gathered all their best warriors together, and all the knights made ready to fight them. The windows of the castle were closed and barred; the air was full of the noise of armor; and the knights were so excited that they could scarcely rest or eat.

Now there was a young knight in the castle, named Sir Roland, who was among those most eager for the battle. He was a splendid warrior, with eyes that shone like stars whenever there

THE MAGIC GARDEN

was anything to do in the way of knightly deeds. And although he was still quite young, his shield had begun to shine enough to show plainly that he had done bravely in some of his errands through the forest. This battle, he thought, would be the great opportunity of his life. And on the morning of the day when they were to go forth to it, and all the knights assembled in the great hall of the castle to receive the commands of their leaders, Sir Roland hoped that he would be put in the most dangerous place of all, so that he could show what knightly stuff he was made of. But when the lord of the castle came to him as he went about in full armor giving his commands, he said: "One brave knight must stay behind and guard the gateway of the castle, and it is you, Sir Roland, being one of the youngest, whom I have chosen for this."

At these words Sir Roland was so disappointed that he bit his lip, and closed his helmet over his face so that the other knights might not see it. For a moment he felt as if he must re-ply angrily to the commander, and tell him that it was not right to leave so sturdy a knight behind, when he was eager to fight. But he struggled against this feeling, and went quietly to look after his duties at the gate.

The gateway was high and narrow, and was reached from outside by a high, narrow bridge that crossed the moat, which surrounded the castle on every side. When an enemy approached, the knight

175

on guard rang a great bell just inside the gate, and the bridge was drawn up against the castle wall, so that no one could come across the moat. So the giants had long ago given up trying to attack the castle itself.

Today the battle was to be in the dark hollow in the forest, and it was not likely that there would be anything to do at the castle gate, except to watch it like a common doorkeeper. It was not strange that Sir Roland thought some one else might have done this.

Presently all the other knights marched out in their flashing armor, their red plumes waving over their heads, and their spears in their hands. The lord of the castle stopped only to tell Sir Roland to keep guard over the gate until they had all returned, and to let no one enter. Then they went into the shadows of the forest, and were soon lost to sight.

Sir Roland stood looking after them long after they had gone, thinking how happy he would be if he were on the way to the battle like them. But after a little he put this out of his mind, and tried to think of pleasanter things. It was a long time before anything happened, or any word came from the battle.

At last Sir Roland saw one of the knights come limping down the path to the castle, and he went out on the bridge to meet him. Now this knight was not a brave one, and he had been frightened away as soon as he was wounded.

"I have been hurt," he said, "so that I cannot fight any more. But I could watch the gate for you, if you would like to go back in my place."

At first Sir Roland's heart leaped with joy, but then he remembered what the commander had told him, and he said:

"I should like to go, but a knight belongs where his commander has put him. My place is here at the gate, and I can not open it even for you. Your place is at the battle."

THE MAGIC GARDEN

DONN P. CRANE

The knight was ashamed when he heard this, and he presently turned about and went into the forest again.

So Sir Roland kept guard silently for another hour. Then there came an old beggar woman down the path to the castle, and asked Sir Roland if she might come in and have some food. He told her that no one could enter the castle that day, but that he would send a servant out to her with food, and that she might sit and rest as long as she would.

"I have been past the hollow in the forest where the battle is going on," said the old woman, while she was waiting.

"And how do you think it is going?" asked Sir Roland.

"Badly for the knights, I am afraid," said the old woman. "The giants are fighting as they have never fought before. I should think you had better go and help your friends."

"I should like to, indeed," said Sir Roland. "But I am set to guard the gateway of the castle, and can not leave."

"One fresh knight would make a great difference when they are all weary with fighting," said the old woman. "I should think that, while there are no enemies about, you would be much more useful there."

"You may well think so," said Sir Roland, "and so may I; but it is neither you nor I that is commander here."

"I suppose," said the old woman then, "that you are one of the kind of knights who like to keep out of fighting. You are lucky to have so good an excuse for staying at home." And she laughed a thin and taunting laugh.

Then Sir Roland was very angry, and thought that if it were only a man instead of a woman, he would show him whether he liked fighting or no. But as it was a woman, he shut his lips and set his teeth hard together, and as the servant came just then with the food he had sent for, he gave it to the old woman quickly, and shut the gate that she might not talk to him any more.

It was not very long before he heard some one calling outside. Sir Roland opened the gate, and saw standing at the other end of the drawbridge a little old man in a long cloak. "Why are you knocking here?" he said. "The castle is closed today."

"Are you Sir Roland?" said the little old man.

"Yes," said Sir Roland.

"Then you ought not to be staying here when your commander and his knights are having so hard a struggle with the giants, and when you have the chance to make yourself the greatest knight in this kingdom. Listen to me! I have brought you a magic sword."

As he said this, the old man drew from under his coat a wonderful sword that flashed in the sunlight as if it were covered with diamonds. "This is the sword of all swords," he said, "and it is for you, if you will leave your idling here by the castle gate, and carry it to the battle. Nothing can stand before it. When you lift it the giants will fall back, your master will be saved, and you will be crowned the victorious knight—the one who will soon take his commander's place as lord of the castle."

Now Sir Roland believed that it was a magician who was

speaking to him, for it certainly appeared to be a magic sword. It seemed so wonderful that the sword should be brought to him, that he reached out his hand as though he would take it, and the little old man came forward, as though he would cross the drawbridge into the castle. But as he did so, it came to Sir Roland's mind again that that bridge and the gateway had been intrusted to him, and he called out "No!" to the old man, so that he stopped where he was standing. But he waved the shining sword in the air again, and said: "It is for you! Take it, and win the victory!"

Sir Roland was really afraid that if he looked any longer at the sword, or listened to any more words of the old man, he would not be able to hold himself within the castle. For this reason he struck the great bell at the gateway, which was the signal for the servants inside to pull in the chains of the drawbridge, and in-

stantly they began to pull, and the drawbridge came up, so that the old man could not cross it to enter the castle, nor Sir Roland to go out.

Then, as he looked across the moat, Sir Roland saw a wonderful thing. The little old man threw off his black cloak, and as he did so he began to grow bigger and bigger, until in a minute more he was a giant as tall as any in the forest. At first Sir Roland could scarcely believe his eyes. Then he real- ized that this must be one of their giant enemies, who had

DONN P. CRANE

changed himself to a little old man through some magic power, that he might make his way into the castle while all the knights were away. Sir Roland shuddered to think what might have happened if he had taken the sword and left the gate unguarded. The giant shook his fist across the moat that lay between them, and then, knowing that he could do nothing more, he went angrily back into the forest.

Sir Roland now resolved not to open the gate again, and to pay no attention to any other visitor. But it was not long before he heard a sound that made him spring forward in joy. It was the bugle of the lord of the castle, and there came sounding after it the bugles of many of the knights that were with him, pealing so joyfully that Sir Roland was sure they were safe and happy. As they came nearer, he could hear their shouts of victory. So he gave the signal to let down the drawbridge again, and went out to meet them. They were dusty and bloodstained and weary, but they had won the battle with the giants; and it had been such a great victory that there had never been a happier home-coming.

Sir Roland greeted them all as they passed in over the bridge and then, when he had closed the gate and fastened it, he followed them into the great hall of the castle. The lord of the castle took his place on the highest seat, with the other knights about him, and Sir Roland came forward with the key of the gate, to give his account of what he had done in the place to which the commander had appointed him. The lord of the castle bowed to him as a sign for him to begin, and just as he opened his mouth to speak, one of the knights cried out:

"The shield! the shield! Sir Roland's shield!"

Every one turned and looked at the shield which Sir Roland carried on his left arm. He himself could see only the top of it, and did not know what they could mean. But what they saw was the golden star of knighthood, shining brightly from the center of Sir Roland's shield. There had never been such amazement in the castle before.

Sir Roland knelt before the lord of the castle to receive his commands. He still did not know why every one was looking at him so excitedly.

"Speak, Sir Knight," said the commander, as soon as he could find his voice after his surprise, "and tell us all that has happened today at the castle. Have you been attacked? Have any giants come hither? Did you fight them alone?"

"No, my Lord," said Sir Roland. "Only one giant has been here, and he went away silently when he found he could not enter."

Then he told all that had happened through the day.

When he had finished, the knights all looked at one another, but no one spoke a word. Then they looked again at Sir Roland's shield, to make sure that their eyes had not deceived them, and there the golden star was still shining.

After a little silence the lord of the castle spoke.

"Men make mistakes," he said, "but our silver shields are never mistaken. Sir Roland has fought and won the hardest battle of all today."

Then the others all rose and saluted Sir Roland, who was the youngest knight that ever carried the golden star.

David Copperfield and Little Em'ly
Arranged from David Copperfield by Charles Dickens

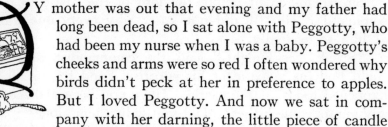

M Y mother was out that evening and my father had long been dead, so I sat alone with Peggotty, who had been my nurse when I was a baby. Peggotty's cheeks and arms were so red I often wondered why birds didn't peck at her in preference to apples. But I loved Peggotty. And now we sat in company with her darning, the little piece of candle with which she waxed her thread, the little house with a thatched roof where the yard measure lived, and Peggotty's work box with a view of St. Paul's cathedral painted on top. I had been reading about crocodiles when Peggotty, after opening her mouth several times without speaking, said at last:

"Master Davy, how should you like to go along with me and spend a fortnight at my brother's at Yarmouth? Wouldn't *that* be a treat?"

"Is your brother an agreeable man, Peggotty?" I inquired.

"Oh, what an agreeable man he is!" cried Peggotty, holding up her hands. "Then there's the sea! And the boats and ships! And the fishermen! And the beach! And Am to play with!"

Peggotty meant her nephew Ham. But she was always leaving off H's when she should have put them on and putting them on when she should have left them off, so she spoke of Ham as though he had been a morsel of English grammar.

I was flushed by her summary of delights, and replied that it would indeed be a treat, but what would my mother say?

"Why then I'll as good as bet a guinea," said Peggotty, "that she'll let us go. I'll ask her, if you like, as soon as ever she comes home."

"But what's she to do while we're away?" said I, putting my small elbows on the table. "She can't live by herself."

"Oh bless you!" said Peggotty, looking at me again. "Don't you know? She's going to stay for a fortnight with Mrs. Grayper."

THE MAGIC GARDEN

Oh! If that was it, I was quite ready to go. I waited, in the utmost impatience until my mother came home, to ascertain if we could get leave to carry out this great idea. Without being nearly so much surprised as I had expected, my mother entered into it readily. It was all arranged that night, and my board and lodging during the visit were to be paid for.

The day soon came for our going. It was such an early day that it came soon, even to me, who was in a fever of expectation, and half afraid that an earthquake or a fiery mountain, or some other great convulsion of nature might interpose to stop the expedition. We were to go in a carrier's cart which departed in the morning after breakfast. I would have given any money to have been allowed to wrap myself up over night, and sleep in my hat and boots.

I am glad to recollect that when the carrier's cart was at the gate, and my mother stood there kissing me, a grateful fondness for her and for the old place I had never turned my back upon before, made me cry. I am glad to know that my mother cried too, and that I felt her heart beat against mine.

The carrier's horse was the laziest horse in the world, I should hope, and shuffled along with his head down, as if he liked to keep the people waiting to whom the packages were directed. I fancied, indeed, that he sometimes chuckled over this reflection, but the carrier said he was only troubled with a cough.

The carrier had a way of keeping his head down, like his horse, and of drooping sleepily forward as he drove, with one of his arms on each of his knees. I say "drove," but it struck me that the cart would have gone to Yarmouth quite as well without him, for the horse did all that—and as to conversation, he had no idea of it but whistling.

Peggotty had a basket of refreshments on her knee, which would have lasted us out handsomely, if we had been going as

far as London in that same conveyance. We ate a good deal, and slept a good deal. Peggotty always went to sleep with her chin upon the handle of the basket, her hold of which never relaxed, and I could not have believed unless I had heard her do it, that one woman could have snored so much.

We made so many turns up and down lanes, and were such a long time delivering a bedstead at a public house, and calling at other places, that I was quite tired, and very glad, when we saw Yarmouth. It looked rather spongy and soppy, I thought, as I carried my eye over the great dull waste that lay across the river; and I could not help wondering, if the world were really as round as my geography-book said, how any part of it came to be so flat. As we drew a little nearer, and saw all the land round about lying a straight low line under the sky, I hinted to Peggotty that a mound or so might have improved it. But Peggotty said, with greater emphasis than usual, that we must take things as we found them, and that, for her part, she was proud to call herself a Yarmouth Bloater.

When we got into the street (which was strange enough to me) and smelt the fish, and pitch, and oakum, and tar, and saw the sailors walking about, and the carts jingling up and down over the stones, I felt that I had done so busy a place an injustice, and said as much to Peggotty, who heard my expressions of delight with great satisfaction, and told me it was well known (I suppose to those who had the good fortune to be born Bloaters) that Yarmouth was, upon the whole, the finest place in the universe.

"Here's my Am!" screamed Peggotty. "Growed out of knowledge!"

He was waiting for us, in fact, at the public-house, and asked me how I found myself, like an old acquaintance. He was a huge, strong fellow of six feet high, broad in proportion, and round-shouldered; but with a simpering boy's face, and curly light hair, that gave him quite a sheepish look. He was dressed in a canvas jacket, and a pair of such very stiff trousers that they would have stood quite as well alone, without any legs in them.

Ham carrying a small box of ours under his arm, and Peggotty carrying another small box of ours, we turned down lanes littered with bits of chips and little hillocks of sand, and went past gas-works, rope-walks, boat-builders' yards, shipwrights' yards, ship-breakers' yards, calkers' yards, riggers' lofts, smiths' forges, and a great many of such places, until we came out upon the dull waste I had already seen at a distance; when Ham said, "Yon's our house, Master Davy!"

I looked in all directions, as far as I could stare over the wilderness, and away at the sea, and away at the river, but no house could I make out. There was a barge, or some other kind of old boat, not far off, high and dry on the ground, with an iron funnel sticking out of it for a chimney and smoking very cosily.

But nothing else in the way of a house that was visible to *me*.

"That's not it?" said I, "that ship-looking thing?"

"That's it, Master Davy," returned Ham.

If it had been Aladdin's Palace, roc's egg and all, I suppose I could not have been more charmed with the romantic idea of living in it. There was a delightful door cut in the side, and it was roofed in, and there were little windows in it; but the wonderful charm of it was, that it was a real boat which had no doubt been upon the water hundreds of times, and which had never been intended to be lived in, on dry land. That was the captivation of it to me. If it had ever been meant to be lived in, I might have thought it small, or inconvenient, or lonely, but never having been designed for any such use, it became a perfect dwelling.

It was beautifully clean inside, and as tidy as possible. There was a table, and a Dutch clock, and a chest of drawers, and on the chest of drawers there was a tea-tray with a painting on it of a lady with a parasol, taking a walk with a military-looking child who was trundling a hoop. The tray was kept from tumbling down, by a Bible, and the tray, if it had tumbled down, would have smashed a quantity of cups and saucers and a teapot that were grouped around the book. On the walls there were some common colored pictures, framed and glazed, of Scripture subjects—Abraham in red going to sacrifice Isaac in blue, and Daniel in yellow cast into a den of green lions. Over the little mantelshelf, was a picture of the Sarah Jane Lugger, built at Sunderland, with a real little wooden stern stuck on to it. There were some hooks in the beams of the ceiling, the use of which I did not understand then; and some lockers and boxes, which served for seats, and filled out the shortage of chairs.

All this I saw in the first glance after I crossed the threshold, and then Peggotty opened a little door and showed me my own bedroom.

It was the completest and most desirable bedroom ever seen, in the stern of the vessel. It had a little window where the rudder used to go through; a little looking-glass, just the right height for me, nailed against the wall, and framed with oyster shells; a little bed which there was just room enough to get into; and a nosegay of seaweed in a blue mug on the table. The walls were whitewashed as white as milk, and the patchwork counterpane made my eyes quite ache with its brightness.

One thing I particularly noticed in this delightful house, was the smell of fish; which was so searching that when I took out my pocket-handkerchief to wipe my nose, I found it smelt exactly as if it had wrapped up a lobster.

On my telling Peggotty of this discovery, she informed me that her brother dealt in lobsters, crabs, and crawfish; and I afterwards found that a heap of these creatures, wonderfully jumbled up together, and never leaving off pinching whatever they laid hold of, were usually to be found in a little outhouse where the pots and kettles were kept.

We were welcomed by a very civil woman in a white apron, whom I had seen curtseying at the door when I was about a quarter of a mile off. Likewise by a most beautiful little girl (or I thought her so) with a necklace of blue beads on, who wouldn't let me kiss her when I offered to, but ran away and hid herself.

By-and-by, when we had dined in a sumptuous manner off boiled dabs, melted butter, and potatoes, with a chop for me, a hairy man with a very good-natured face, came home. As he called Peggotty "Lass," and gave her a hearty smack on the cheek, I had no doubt that he was her brother. And so he turned out to be, for presently Peggotty, turning to me, introduced him to me as Mr. Peggotty.

"Glad to see you, Sir," said Mr. Peggotty. "You'll find us rough, Sir, but you'll find us ready."

I thanked him, and replied that I was sure I should be happy in such a delightful place.

"How's your Ma, Mrs. Copperfield?" said Mr. Peggotty. "Did you leave her pretty jolly?"

I gave Mr. Peggotty to understand that she was as jolly as I could wish.

"Well, Sir, if you can make out here, fur a fortnut, 'long wi' her," nodding at his sister, "and Ham, and little Em'ly, we shall be proud of your company."

Having done the honors of his house in this hospitable manner, Mr. Peggotty went out to wash himself in a kettleful of hot water, remarking that "cold would never get *his* muck off." He soon returned, greatly improved in appearance, but so ruddy, that I couldn't help thinking his face had this in common with the lobsters, crabs, and crawfish;—that it went into the hot water very black, and came out very red.

After tea, when the door was shut and all was made snug (the nights being cold and misty now) it seemed to me the most

delicious retreat that could ever be imagined. To hear the wind getting up out at sea, to know that the fog was creeping over the desolate flat outside, and to look at the fire, and think that there was no house near but this one, and this one a boat, was like enchantment. Little Em'ly had overcome her shyness, and was sitting by my side upon the lowest and least of the lockers, which was just large enough for us two, and just fitted into the chimney corner. Mrs. Peggotty with the white apron, was knitting on the opposite side of the fire. Peggotty at her needle-work was as much at home with Saint Paul's and the bit of wax-candle as if they had never known any other roof. Ham was trying to recollect a scheme of telling fortunes with the dirty cards, and printing off fishy impressions of his thumb on all the cards he turned. Mr. Peggotty was smoking his pipe. I felt it was a time for conversation.

"Mr. Peggotty!" says I.

"Sir," says he.

"Did you give your son the name of Ham, because you lived in a sort of Ark?"

Mr. Peggotty seemed to think it a deep idea, but answered: "No, Sir. I never giv him no name."

"Who did give him that name, then?" said I.

"Why, Sir, his father giv it him," said Mr. Peggotty.

"I thought you were his father!"

"My brother Joe was *his* father," said Mr. Peggotty.

"Dead, Mr. Peggotty?" I hinted, after a respectful pause.

"Drowndead," said Mr. Peggotty.

I was very much surprised that Mr. Peggotty was not Ham's father, and began to wonder whether I was mistaken about his relationship to anybody else there. I was so curious to know, that I made up my mind to have it out with Mr. Peggotty.

"Little Em'ly," I said, glancing at her. "She is your daughter, isn't she, Mr. Peggotty?"

"No, Sir. My brother-in-law, Tom, was *her* father."

I couldn't help it. "—Dead, Mr. Peggotty?" I hinted, after another respectful silence.

"Drowndead," said Mr. Peggotty.

"Haven't you *any* children, Mr. Peggotty?"

"No, master," he answered, with a short laugh. "I'm a bacheldore."

"A bachelor!" I said, astonished. "Why, who's that, Mr. Peggotty?" pointing to the person in the apron who was knitting.

"That's Missis Gummidge," said Mr. Peggotty.

"Gummidge, Mr. Peggotty?"

But at this point, Peggotty—I mean my own peculiar Peggotty—made such impressive motions to me not to ask any further questions, that I could only sit and look at all the silent company, until it was time to go to bed. Then, in the privacy of my own little cabin, she informed me that Ham and Em'ly were an orphan nephew and niece, whom my host had at different times adopted in their childhood when they were left destitute; and that Mrs. Gummidge was the widow of his partner in a boat, who had died very poor. He was but a poor man himself, said Peggotty, but as good as gold and as true as steel. The only subject, she informed me, on which he ever showed a violent temper or swore an oath, was this generosity of his; and if it were ever referred to, by any one of them, he struck the table a heavy blow with his right hand (had split it on one such occasion), and swore a dreadful oath that he would be "gormed" if he didn't cut and run away for good, if it was ever mentioned again. It appeared, in answer to my inquiries, that nobody had the least idea of the meaning of this terrible word "to be gormed"; but that they all regarded it as a most solemn oath.

I was very sensible of my entertainer's goodness, and listened to the women's going to bed in another little crib like mine at the opposite end of the boat, and to him and Ham hanging up two hammocks for themselves on the hooks I had noticed in the roof. As slumber gradually stole upon me, I heard the wind howling out at sea and coming on across the flat so fiercely, that I had a lazy apprehension of the great deep rising in the night. But I bethought myself that I was in a boat, after all, and that a man like Mr. Peggotty was not a bad person to have on board if any thing did happen. Nothing happened, however, worse than morning. Almost as soon as it shone upon the oyster shell frame of my mirror, I was out of bed, and out with little Em'ly, picking up stones upon the beach.

"You're quite a sailor, I suppose?" I said to Em'ly. I don't know that I supposed any thing of the kind, but I felt it an act of gallantry to say something.

"No," replied Em'ly, shaking her head. "I'm afraid of the sea."

"Afraid!" I said, with an air of boldness, and looking very big at the mighty ocean. "*I'm* not!"

"Ah! but it's cruel," said Em'ly. "I have seen it tear a boat as big as our house, all to pieces."

"I hope it wasn't the boat that—"

"That father was drownded in?" said Em'ly. "No. Not that one, I never see that boat."

"Nor him?" I asked her.

Little Em'ly shook her head. "Not to remember!"

Here was a point of likeness in our two lives! I immediately went into an explanation how I had never seen my own father, and how my mother and I had always lived by ourselves in the happiest state imaginable, and always meant to live so.

"But," said Em'ly, as she looked about for shells and pebbles, "your father was a gentleman and your mother is a lady; and my father was a fisherman, and my mother was a fisherman's daughter, and my Uncle Dan is a fisherman."

THE MAGIC GARDEN

"Dan is Mr. Peggotty, is he?" said I. "He must be very good, I should think?"

"Good?" said Em'ly. "If I was ever to be a lady, I'd give him a sky-blue coat with diamond buttons, nankeen trousers, a red velvet waistcoat, a cocked hat, a large gold watch, a silver pipe, and a box of money."

I said I had no doubt that Mr. Peggotty well-deserved these treasures. I must acknowledge that I felt it difficult to picture him quite at his ease in the raiment proposed for him by his grateful little niece and that I was particularly doubtful about the cocked hat, but I kept these sentiments to myself.

"You would like to be a lady?" I said.

Em'ly looked at me, and laughed, and nodded "yes."

"I should like it very much. We would all be gentlefolks together, then, me, and Uncle, and Ham, and Mrs. Gummidge, and we'd help the poor fishermen with money when they come to any hurt."

This seemed to me to be a very satisfactory picture. I expressed my pleasure in it, and little Em'ly was emboldened to say shyly: "Don't you think you are afraid of the sea, now?"

It was quiet enough to reassure me, but I have no doubt if I had seen a moderately large wave come tumbling in, I should have taken to my heels. However, I said, "No!" and I added, "You don't seem to be, either, though you say you are." For she was walking much too near the brink of a sort of old jetty or wooden causeway we had strolled upon and I was afraid of her falling over.

"I'm not afraid in this way," said little Em'ly. "But I wake when it blows and tremble to think of Uncle Dan and Ham, and believe I hear 'em crying out for help. But I'm not afraid in this way. Not a bit. Look here!"

193

She started from my side, and ran along a jagged timber which protruded from the place we stood upon, and overhung the deep water at some height, without the least defence, springing forward to her destruction (as it appeared to me). I uttered a cry, but directly the light, bold, fluttering little figure turned and came back safe to me, and I soon laughed at my fears.

We strolled a long way, and loaded ourselves with things that we thought curious, and put some stranded star-fish carefully back into the water, then made our way home to Mr. Peggotty's dwelling. We stopped under the lee of the lobster out-house to exchange an innocent kiss, and went in to breakfast glowing with health and pleasure.

"Like two young mavishes," Mr. Peggotty said. I knew this meant, in our local dialect, like two young thrushes, and received it as a compliment.

Of course I was in love with little Em'ly. My fancy raised up something round that blue-eyed mite of a child, which made a very angel of her. If, any sunny forenoon, she had spread a little pair of wings and flown away before my eyes, I don't think I should have regarded it as much more than I had had reason to expect. We used to walk about that dim old flat at Yarmouth in a loving manner, hours and hours. The days sported by us, as if Time had not grown up himself yet, but were a child too, and always at play.

We were the admiration of Mrs. Gummidge and Peggotty, who used to whisper of an evening when we sat, lovingly, on our little locker side by side, "Lor! wasn't it beautiful!" Mr. Peggotty smiled at us from behind his pipe, and Ham grinned all the evening and did nothing else.

I soon found out that Mrs. Gummidge did not always make herself so agreeable as she might have been expected to do, in consideration of the kindness with which Mr. Peggotty had taken

her in. Mrs. Gummidge's was rather a fretful disposition, and
she whimpered more sometimes than was comfortable for other
parties in so small an establishment. I was very sorry for her,
but there were moments when it would have been more agreeable, I thought, if Mrs. Gummidge had had a convenient apartment of her own to retire to, and had stopped there until her
spirits revived.

Mr. Peggotty went occasionally to a public house called
The Willing Mind. I discovered this, by his being out on the
second or third evening of our visit, and by Mrs. Gummidge's
looking up at the Dutch clock, between eight and nine, and
saying he was there, and that, what was more, she had known
in the morning he would go there.

Mrs. Gummidge had been in a low state all day, and had
burst into tears in the forenoon, when the fire smoked. "I am
a lone lorn creetur'," were Mrs. Gummidge's words, when that
unpleasant occurrence took place, "and every think goes contrairy with me."

"Oh, it'll soon leave off," said Peggotty—I again mean our Peggotty—"and besides, it's not more disagreeable to you than to us."

"I feel it more," said Mrs. Gummidge.

It was a very cold day, with cutting blasts of wind. Mrs.
Gummidge's peculiar corner of the fireside seemed to me to be
the warmest and snuggest in the place, as her chair was certainly
the easiest, but it didn't suit her that day at all. She was con-
stantly complaining of the cold, and of its occasioning what
she called "the creeps in her back." At last she shed tears on
that subject, and said again that she was "a lone lorn creetur'
and every think went contrairy with her."

"It is certainly very cold," said Peggotty. "Everybody
must feel it."

"I feel it more than other people," said Mrs. Gummidge.

So at dinner, when Mrs. Gummidge was always helped immediately after me, to whom the preference was given as a visitor of distinction, the fish were small and bony, and the potatoes were a little burnt. We all acknowledged that we felt this something of a disappointment; but Mrs. Gummidge said she felt it more than we did, and shed tears again.

Accordingly, when Mr. Peggotty came home about nine o'clock, this unfortunate Mrs. Gummidge was knitting in her corner in a very wretched and miserable condition. Peggotty had been working cheerfully. Ham had been patching up a great pair of water-boots, and I, with little Em'ly by my side, had been reading to them. Mrs. Gummidge had never made any other remark than a forlorn sigh, and had never raised her eyes since tea.

"Well, Mates," said Mr. Peggotty, taking his seat, "and how are you?"

We all said something, or looked something, to welcome him, except Mrs. Gummidge, who shook her head over her knitting.

"What's amiss?" said Mr. Peggotty, with a clap of his hands. "Cheer up, old Mawther." (Mr. Peggotty meant old girl.)

Mrs. Gummidge did not appear to be able to cheer up. She took out an old black silk handkerchief and wiped her eyes, but instead of putting it in her pocket, kept it out, and wiped them again, and still kept it out ready for use.

"What's amiss, dame?" said Mr. Peggotty.

"Nothing," returned Mrs. Gummidge. "You've come from The Willing Mind, Dan'l?"

"Why yes, I've took a short spell at The Willing Mind to-night," said Mr. Peggotty.

"I'm sorry I should drive you there," said Mrs. Gummidge.

"Drive! I don't want no driving," returned Mr. Peggotty, with an honest laugh. "I only go too ready."

"Very ready," said Mrs. Gummidge, shaking her head, and wiping her eyes. "Yes, yes, very ready. I am sorry it should be along of me that you're so ready."

"Along o' you. It ain't along o' you!" said Mr. Peggotty. "Don't ye believe a bit on it."

"Yes, yes, it is," cried Mrs. Gummidge. "I know what I am. I know that I'm a lone lorn creetur, and not only that every think goes contrairy with me, but that I go contrairy with everybody. Yes, yes. I feel more than other people do, and I show it more. It's my misfortun'."

I really couldn't help thinking as I sat taking in all this, that it was a misfortune for other members of that family besides Mrs. Gummidge. But Mr. Peggotty made no such retort, only answering with another entreaty to Mrs. Gummidge to cheer up.

"I ain't what I could wish myself to be," said Mrs. Gummidge. "I am far from it. I know what I am. My troubles has made me contrairy. I feel my troubles, and they make me contrairy. I wish I didn't feel 'em, but I do. I wish I could be hardened to 'em, but I ain't. I make the house uncomfortable. I've made your sister so all day, and Master Davy."

Here I was suddenly melted, and roared out, "No, you haven't, Mrs. Gummidge," in great mental distress.

"It's far from right that I should do it," said Mrs. Gummidge. "It ain't a fit return. I had better go into the Poorhouse and die. I am a lone lorn creetur, and had much better not make myself contrairy here!"

Mrs. Gummidge retired with these words, and betook herself to bed. When she was gone, Mr. Peggotty, who had not exhibited a trace of any feeling but the profoundest sympathy, looked round upon us, and nodding his head with a lively expression of pity still animating his face, said in a whisper: "She's been thinking of the old 'un." I did not quite understand what Old One Mrs. Gummidge was supposed to have fixed her mind upon, until Peggotty, on seeing me to bed, explained that it was the late Mr. Gummidge, and that her brother always took that for a received truth on such occasions, and that it always had a moving effect upon him. Some time after he was in his hammock that night, I heard him myself repeat to Ham, "Poor thing! She's been thinking of the old 'un!" And whenever Mrs. Gummidge was overcome in a similar manner during the remainder of our stay (which happened some few times) he always said the same thing in explanation of the circumstance, and always with the tenderest pity.

So the fortnight slipped away, varied by nothing but the variation of the tide, which altered Mr. Peggotty's times of going out and coming in, and altered Ham's engagements also. When the latter was unemployed, he sometimes walked with us to show us the boats and ships, and once or twice he took us for a row. I never hear the name, or read the name, of Yarmouth, but I am reminded of a certain Sunday morning on the beach, the bells ringing for church, little Em'ly leaning on my shoulder, Ham lazily dropping stones into the water, and the sun, away at sea, just breaking through the heavy mist, and showing us the ships, like their own shadows.

At last the day came for going home. I bore up against the separation from Mr. Peggotty and Mrs. Gummidge, but my sorrow at leaving little Em'ly was piercing. We went arm in arm to the public house where the carrier put up, and I promised, on the road, to write to her. (I kept that promise afterwards in letters larger than those in which apartments are usually announced as being to let.) We were greatly overcome at parting, and if ever, in my life, I have had a void made in my heart, I had one made that day.

Gigi and the Magic Ring*

An Italian Fairy Tale

ANNE MACDONELL

"I'll make you rich and happy yet," said Gigi (Jeejee) to his mother. "But first I must go out into the world. Maria, my sister, will take care of you while I am gone; and remember if you hear nothing of me for a time, no news is good news."

So off he went; and soon he had to pass through a town. Do you think he lost sight of poor folks there? Not a bit of it! The very first person he set eyes on was an old woman bending under the weight of a heavy oil jar she was carrying. "I wouldn't let my old grandmother carry that," said Gigi. "Here!" he cried, "give it to me." And he took the jar from her, swung it upon his shoulder, and bore it up the steep street at the top of which she lived, and set it down in her kitchen.

"Thank you, my fine young man," said the old woman, "and may good luck go with you! Will you sit down and rest a while? My place is poor, but you are right welcome."

"I have a long way before me," replied Gigi, "but a seat in your chimney corner for a minute or two I will not refuse." And he sat down and played with the dog and cat that lay before the fire.

"And where are you going, my fine young man?"

"Into the world," he answered.

"A place full of wonders, to be sure, but the road will be a bit lonesome for you. Have you no friend to go along with you?"

"No," replied Gigi.

"Then what do you say to taking my dog and cat? They are wiser than their kind, and their company might hearten you on the road."

*From *The Italian Fairy Book*, published by Frederick A. Stokes Company.

"That would it now," said the young man. "Fine company they would be! Thank you, good mistress."

"Three mouths to feed instead of one, 'tis true," she went on; "and sometimes the tables of the world are poorly spread. But should that happen, I have something here will help you." She went to a cupboard and brought out a ring.

"Take this," she said, "and when you want anything very much, wear it on your finger and turn it about. Then you'll see what you'll see! Never lose it or give it away, or let it be stolen or changed. For then you will be worse off than ever, and the ring might get into bad hands."

"It is too much," said Gigi politely. He knew nothing at all about jewelry and thought it was probably a poor kind of thing; but to accept it seemed like robbing a poor old woman. However, she insisted, and when he bade her good-bye the ring was in his pocket. Soon he had forgotten all about it. The dog and the cat were running along or capering about him in wild glee. When they had left the town miles behind them, the night clouds began to gather, and Gigi looked out for a place to sleep. There were no houses in sight, but there was thick wood.

"We can enter here without rapping at any man's door," said Gigi. So they made the wood their inn and all three snuggled down together and tried to go to sleep. But sleep was impossible to Gigi. He was too hungry.

"This would be the best place in all the world," he said, "if only there was something to eat. I wish—oh, I wish a table could be set before me now, with a fine supper on it." His fingers had been playing with the ring in his pocket. Now he put it on, and he was twisting and turning it about, when all at once his wish came true! It was not too dark but that he could see close by him a table spread with a fine cloth, with dishes, forks, knives and spoons, and hot, smoking roast duck on it, and delicious

THE MAGIC GARDEN

fruit, and more things than he had ever had for supper before.

"Oh-h-h!" he said. The dog and the cat sat up, their noses in the air. It wasn't real, of course. It couldn't be. He touched it. It was real. He smelt it. The dog and cat sniffed too and grew excited. He tasted. Oh, now there was no doubt about it! Everything was real—and so good! He ate and he drank, and the dog and cat ate along with him; and they were all three as merry as possible over their banquet in the woods.

"The old woman must have been a fairy," he said to himself. That was a ring indeed she had given him. What should he wish for next? He thought of hundreds of things—gold and silver, fine clothes for himself and his mother and Maria, horses and carriages, guns and swords; but the wishes came tumbling on top of each other, head over heels and all fell in a jumbled heap.

"How stupid I am," said Gigi, "I can't imagine what I wish for most. Well, I've often heard that people lose their heads when good luck comes their way; but I'd like to keep mine on my shoulders." Then he lay down again on the bed of leaves, without wishing for anything, and the dog was at his head and the cat at his feet; and they all fell fast asleep.

He woke next morning early, and was up and astir, with the dog and the cat at his heels; and everything about him shone and sang. There was nothing so fine in all the world as stepping out into the fresh morning world. Was he wishing for horses and carriages? He laughed at the idea. Two good legs and a sapling from the wood where he had slept, were better than the King's state coach. Up hill and down dale, through wood and field, by stream and meadow he went, easily, cheerily, and his two good friends were the best of company.

At last he came to a fine palace built on the roadside; and out of an upper window looked a beautiful maiden, and she smiled as Gigi passed below.

"Oh, I could look at her all day long!" he said. "But she would never speak to a poor boy like me," he sighed. "Oh, I wish—;" and as he said the word, he remembered he could have whatever he wanted in the world. The ring was on his finger on the instant; and he turned it about as he said, "I want a fine mansion, but much finer it must be than the one that lovely girl is looking out of. And I want it just opposite hers."

In a twinkling he stood, no longer in the open road, but in a great palace, more splendid than any he had ever seen; and when he looked out at the window, there was a maiden at the window opposite, and smiling, quite plainly smiling at him. Yet he was still Gigi, in his old clothes with the dust of the road on them; and his dog and his cat were there at his heels. Well, decidedly it was a ring worth having! He wished for fine clothes. They were on his back. For servants. They came at his call. For meat and drink. He did not know the names of all the fine things that were set before him.

"Perhaps she would speak to me now," he said. There was no doubt about that. The very next morning her father and mother came and called on him, and said they wished to make the acquaintance of their new neighbor, who was evidently an eminent gentleman. They could hardly take their eyes off his fine furniture, his fine clothes, and the gold chain he wore about his neck. They flattered him a great deal; and Gigi thought they were very amiable people indeed.

Next day he returned their call, and received a cordial welcome. He was presented to their only daughter, Maliarda, and the two young people quickly made friends. Before the day was over Gigi had asked her hand in marriage, and her parents, who thought he must be at least a great prince, or favored by an enchanter, were only too glad to consent. They thought Gigi would be very useful to them.

DONN P. CRANE

Now, on the eve of the wedding-day they all paid a visit to Gigi, and while they talked together, Maliarda asked him to tell her how it came about that his splendid house had sprung up so suddenly. He was the simplest, truthfullest lad in the world; and so he told her all about his journeying into the world, his meeting with the old woman, her present of the ring, and everything that followed. "And do you keep that precious ring always on your finger?" she asked. "Always!" he replied. "Night and day, waking and sleeping."

She whispered the secret to her mother. When they were having supper, the mother poured something from a phial into Gigi's wine while his back was turned, and into the plates of his dog and cat under the table. It was a sleep-drink she had given them; and soon after Gigi's eyes began to close, and the cat and dog slept and snored.

"Your lord is weary after hunting," said the father to the servant who was waiting. "Carry him to that couch; and we will take our leave." Then he called all the servants together and said, "Come to my house. I have your master's orders to instruct you in your duties tomorrow." And they followed him out of the palace. But Maliarda stayed behind a moment; going up to Gigi, as he lay in a deep sleep, she took the ring from his finger and fled. His dog and cat were too drowsy to warn him.

Once out of the house, she put the ring on her finger, and as she turned it, she said, "I wish that lord Gigi's palace be moved to the highest, steepest, snowiest peak of yonder mountain range!" And on the instant the palace was removed to where she had decreed. Maliarda ran back to her parents' house and told what had happened. They feigned surprise, and turning to the servants, informed them of the vanishing of their master's house, and said, "Your master must have been an evil magician. He has played a cruel trick on you. What an escape our daughter has had!" Then they gave the servants money and dismissed them.

When Gigi awoke next morning he was shivering and shaking. Where was he? In his own palace, though evidently he had not gone to bed. And there were his two friends the dog and the cat. But why was he so cold? He got up, walked to the window, and looked out, expecting to see the palace of his neighbors, and perhaps thinking to catch a glimpse of Maliarda. This was his wedding day! But all familiar things had vanished, and he saw only mountain peaks and snow and sky. What did it mean? He rang the bell violently. No one answered. He called for his valet, for his butler, for his cook, for his coachman. Nobody came. The house was quite still. He searched upstairs and downstairs, and found he was alone in his palace save for the dog and cat, and on the top of the highest mountain peak. Beneath him could be seen only ice, snow, and terrible precipices!

"Who has done this to me?" he cried. "Have I an enemy? Well, what does it matter? I have only to wish myself down and turn my ring." But his ring was gone! Who was the thief? He tried to recall what had happened. He had been very sleepy at supper time. He did not remember getting up from the table or bidding his guests good-night. And only one person knew the value of the ring—! Oh, could his beautiful Maliarda be a traitor?

Impossible to get down the mountain. There was no path; and if he tried to make one, he would perish in the snow, or roll over into some terrible precipice. And there was not two days' food in all the palace!

Now the dog and the cat were sorely troubled at their master's sadness, and soon they found out the reason of it. "Have patience, dear master," they said. "Where a man dare not walk, we can. Give us a day, and see if we do not get back your ring."

"You are my only hope," answered Gigi. He fed them well, and then opened the door for them. So the dog and cat set off, and they slipped, and slid, and crawled, and hung on, and climbed and sprang, and helped each other, and never stopped till they were down on the green plain. There they came to a river. The cat sat on the dog's back, and the dog swam across.

At last they came to the palace of the faithless Maliarda. By this time it was night, and the household were all in bed and asleep. Of course all doors and windows were barred; but in the back door was a little cat-hole; and they squeezed through one after the other. Then said the cat to the dog, "Stay you here and keep guard. I will go upstairs and see what can be done." She slipped up and went to the door of Maliarda's room. But the door was shut, and there was no little hole to

 creep through. The cat sat down and thought and thought; and as she sat there thinking, a little mouse ran across the floor. The cat smelt her in the dark, put out a paw and caught her. What a delicious mouthful she would be! But the mouse squeaked out piteously, and begged that her life might be saved. "Very well," said the cat; "but in return you must promise to gnaw a hole in that door opposite, for I have business inside."

The mouse began to gnaw; and she gnawed as hard as she could. She gnawed and she gnawed till all her teeth were broken; and still the hole was so little she couldn't get in herself, let alone the cat.

"Have you any young ones?" said the cat to the mouse.

"Oh yes, I have seven or eight, the finest little family ever you saw."

"Bring me the littlest, then." And the mouse ran away, and came back with a tiny mite of a mousikin.

Then said the cat to the little mousikin, "Now be quick and clever and you'll save your mother's life. Get in through that hole; creep into the lady's bed, and take off the ring from her finger. If you can't get it, bite her finger softly, and she'll take off the ring herself without waking. Then bring it to me."

Mousikin ran in, but in a minute she was back again.

"The lady has no ring on her finger," she cheeped.

"Then it is in her mouth. Go again; creep into her bed; hit her nose with your tail. She will open her mouth and the ring will drop out. Bring it here to me, and you'll have saved your mother's life."

Off ran mousikin, and in another minute she was back with the ring. The mice scurried back to their holes. The cat slipped down the stairs, made a sign to the dog, and they both crept out through the hole in the back door.

THE MAGIC GARDEN

"Oh, how pleased our master will be," said the cat.

But the dog was not in a good humor. He was the bigger, and he would have liked to have found the ring and carried it back to Gigi himself. So when they came once more to the river, he said, "If you give me the ring, I'll carry you across." But the cat refused. They quarrelled, and the ring fell into the river. On the instant a fish snapped at it as if it had been a pretty fly. But the dog jumped in, and dived for the fish, caught it and got the ring from its mouth. Then he said to the cat in a grand manner, "Jump on my back, pussy, and I will carry you across." The cat obeyed, but very sulkily; and soon they were on the other side. Not a word did they say to each other that was not angry and quarrelsome all the way up the mountain. The sun had risen by the time they reached the top; and there was their master waiting for them at the palace door.

"Have you the ring?" he cried. And the dog dropped it at his feet.

"But 'twas I got it back. By my cleverness, all alone, I got it back," cried the cat.

"How could you ever have reached the place at all had I not carried you over the river?" roared the dog.

"But 'twas I caught the mouse that gnawed the hole—!"

And the dog broke in growling, "It was the least you could do after the trouble I took."

"Dear friends! dear friends!" said Gigi, "do not quarrel! You have both been brave and clever and faithful. You have saved my life between you. I love one as much as the other." And with one hand he caressed the dog, and with the other the cat, and took them into the palace and fed them both. Then they were both the best of friends again, and told their master all their adventures by the way. "Now," said Gigi, "we'll say good-bye to this mountain." He put the ring on his finger, turned it and said, "I wish my palace to descend to the plain and the palace of the faithless Maliarda and her parents to be up here among the ice and snow!"

Next moment both wishes were fulfilled. He was down in the green and flowering plain; and the wicked three in their palace were up on the freezing mountain-top.

Did they ever get down any more? Well, I have heard that Gigi had a little mercy on them after some days of anger. He turned his ring, and wished the faithless three half-way down, whence they could scramble to the level, where trees grew and where there were some scattered huts. But their palace was left up on the top; and much good did it do them there! He never saw them again.

As for Gigi, he soon tired of his fine palace; and when a year and a day had passed from the time he left home, he said to his trusty companions,

"Come, my friends, we'll take to the road again. I have a longing to see my mother and my sister Maria." So he turned back to his own village. On his way he passed through the town where he had met the old woman who had given him the ring, but he could not find her nor hear any news of her. So he hurried on home.

His mother and sister hardly knew him again. That fine young man with the grand clothes their Gigi! Not possible!

"Have you found fortune already, my son?"

"I carry it on my finger." He laughed, and held out the ring.

"Very pretty," said his mother. "But instead of chattering here I should be getting ready your dinner. And nothing you like in the house! Make haste, Maria!"

"Don't trouble," said Gigi. "See what a fine cook I have become!" And there in the middle of the kitchen stood a table loaded with good things to eat—macaroni and roast goose, and grapes and oranges and wine.

"Oh-h-h-h!" cried the two women.

"Sit down and eat," said the young man, "and I'll tell you all my adventures."

They sat down; he loaded their plates; but they could hardly swallow a mouthful for their wonder at all Gigi told them. When he came to the tale of Maliarda's deceit, they wept and said he was much better at home with them.

"So I think," replied Gigi; "and I am not sure if the old woman's best gift to me be not my good friends here under the table."

"To be sure!" said his mother. "What should a strong hearty young fellow like you do with an enchanted ring? Fine mischief it has got you into already! Give it to me, and I'll hide it away in my wedding-chest among the best sheets and the winter coverlets. With the money you have on you, you can set up for yourself."

"That is so," he replied, "And if the old wife were to pass by one day, who knows but I might give her the ring back again."

Is the ring still in the wedding-chest? Does Gigi ever take it out, put it on his finger and wish? I do not know. When I have passed his way I have seen him ploughing with a fine team of fat oxen, and singing the while, or in the woods with his good friends the cat and dog, for they are still alive and hearty. He has not yet gone back to live in a palace; but all the neighbors envy his mother her good son Gigi.

The Golden Touch
NATHANIEL HAWTHORNE

Once upon a time, there lived a very rich man, and a king besides, whose name was Midas; and he had a little daughter, whom nobody but myself ever heard of, and whose name I either never knew, or have entirely forgotten. So, because I love odd names for little girls, I choose to call her Marygold.

This King Midas was fonder of gold than anything else in the world. If he loved anything better, or half so well, it was the one little maiden who played so merrily around her father's footstool. But the more Midas loved his daughter, the more did he desire and seek wealth. He thought, foolish man! that the best thing he could possibly do for this dear child would be to bequeath her the immensest pile of yellow, glistening coin, that had ever been heaped together since the world was made. Thus, he gave all his thoughts and time to this one purpose.

And yet, in his earlier days, before he was so entirely possessed of this insane desire for riches, King Midas had shown a great taste for flowers. He planted a garden, in which grew the biggest and beautifullest and sweetest roses that any mortal ever saw or smelt. But now, if he looked at them at all, it was only to calculate how much the garden would be worth if each of the innumerable rose petals were a thin plate of gold.

At length (as people always grow more and more foolish, unless they take care to grow wiser and wiser), Midas had got to be so exceedingly unreasonable that he could scarcely bear to see or touch any object that was not gold. He made it his custom, therefore, to pass large portions of every day in a dark

THE MAGIC GARDEN

and dreary apartment, under ground, at the basement of his palace. It was here that he kept his wealth. Here, after carefully locking the door, he would take a bag of gold coin, or a gold cup as big as a washbowl, or a heavy golden bar, or a peck measure of gold dust, and bring them from the obscure corners of the room into the one bright and narrow sunbeam that fell from the dungeon-like window. He valued the sunbeam for no other reason but that his treasure would not shine without its help. And then would he reckon over the coins in the bag; toss up the bar, and catch it as it came down; sift the gold-dust through his fingers; look at the funny image of his own face, as reflected in the burnished circumference of the cup, and whisper to himself, "O Midas, rich King Midas, what a happy man art thou!" But it was laughable to see how the image of his face kept grinning at him, out of the polished surface of the cup. It seemed to be aware of his foolish behavior, and to have a naughty inclination to make fun of him.

Midas called himself a happy man, but felt that he was not yet quite so happy as he might be. The very tiptop of enjoyment would never be reached, unless the whole world were to become his treasure-room, and be filled with yellow metal which should be all his own.

Midas was enjoying himself in his treasure-room, one day, as usual, when he perceived a shadow fall over the heaps of gold; and, looking suddenly up, what should he behold but the figure of a stranger, standing in the bright and narrow sunbeam! It was a young man, with a cheerful and ruddy face. Whether it was that the imagination of King Midas threw a yellow tinge over everything, or whatever the cause might be, he could not help fancying that the smile with which the stranger regarded him had a kind of golden radiance in it. Certainly, although his figure intercepted the sunshine, there was now a brighter gleam upon all the piled-up treasure than before. Even the remotest corners had their share of it, and were lighted up, when the stranger smiled, as with tips of flame and sparkles of fire.

As Midas knew that he had carefully turned the key in the lock, and that no mortal strength could possibly break into this treasure-room, he, of course, concluded that his visitor must be something more than mortal. Midas had met such beings before now, and was not sorry to meet one of them again. The stranger's aspect, indeed, was so good humoured and kindly, if not beneficent, that it would have been unreasonable to suspect him of intending any mischief. It was far more probable that he came to do Midas a favour. And what could that favour be, unless to multiply his heaps of treasure?

The stranger gazed about the room; and when his lustrous smile had glistened upon all the golden objects that were there he turned again to Midas.

"You are a wealthy man, friend Midas!" he observed. "I doubt whether any other four walls on earth, contain so much gold as you have contrived to pile up in this room."

"I have done pretty well—pretty well," answered Midas, in a discontented tone. "But, after all, it is but a trifle, when you consider that it has taken me my whole life to get it together."

"What!" exclaimed the stranger. "Then you are not satisfied?"

Midas shook his head.

"And pray what would satisfy you?" asked the stranger.

Midas paused and meditated. He felt a presentiment that this stranger, with such a golden luster in his good-humoured smile, had come hither with both the power and the purpose of gratifying his utmost wishes. Now, therefore, was the fortunate moment, when he had but to speak, and obtain whatever it might come into his head to ask. So he thought, and thought, and thought, and heaped up one golden mountain upon another, in his imagination, without being able to imagine them big enough. At last, a bright idea occurred to King Midas. "I am weary of collecting my treasures with so much trouble," said he. "I wish everything that I touch to be changed to gold!"

The stranger's smile grew so very broad, that it seemed to fill the room like an outburst of the sun.

"The Golden Touch!" exclaimed he. "You certainly deserve credit, friend Midas, for striking out so brilliant a conception. But are you quite sure that this will satisfy you?"

"How could it fail?" said Midas.

"And will you never regret the possession of it?"

"I ask nothing else, to render me perfectly happy."

"Be it as you wish, then," replied the stranger, waving his hand in token of farewell. "Tomorrow, at sunrise, you will find yourself gifted with the Golden Touch."

The figure of the stranger then became exceedingly bright, and Midas involuntarily closed his eyes. On opening them again, he beheld only one yellow sunbeam in the room, and, all around him, the glistening of the metal which he had spent his life in hoarding up.

Whether Midas slept as usual that night, the story does not say. Asleep or awake, however, his mind was probably

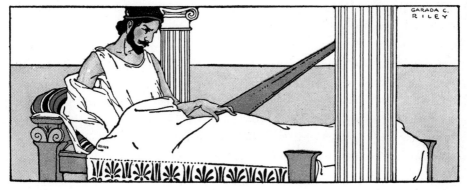

in the state of a child's, to whom a beautiful new plaything has been promised in the morning. At any rate, day had hardly peeped over the hills, when King Midas was broad awake, and, stretching his arms out of bed, began to touch the objects that were within reach, but was grievously disappointed to perceive that they remained of exactly the same substance as before. Indeed, he felt very much afraid that he had only dreamed about the lustrous stranger, or else that the latter had been making game of him.

All this while, it was only the gray of the morning, with but a streak of brightness along the edge of the sky, where Midas could not see it. He lay in a very disconsolate mood, regretting the downfall of his hopes, until the earliest sunbeam shone through the window, and gilded the ceiling over his head. It seemed to Midas that this bright yellow sunbeam was reflected in rather a singular way on the white covering of the bed. Looking more closely, what was his astonishment and delight, when he found that this linen fabric had been transmuted to what seemed a woven texture of the purest and brightest gold! The Golden Touch had come to him with the first sunbeam!

Midas started up, in a kind of joyful frenzy, and ran about the room, grasping at everything that happened to be in his way. He seized one of the bedposts, and it became immediately a fluted golden pillar. He pulled aside a window-curtain, in order to admit a clear spectacle of the wonders which he was performing; and the tassel grew heavy in his hand,—a mass of gold. He took up a book from the table. At his first touch it assumed the appearance of such a splendidly bound and gilt-edged volume as one often meets with nowadays; but, on running his fingers through the leaves, behold! it was a bundle of thin golden plates, in which all the wisdom of the book had grown illegible. He hurriedly put on his clothes, and was enraptured

her eyes, still sobbing as if her heart would break.

"How now, my little lady!" cried Midas. "Pray what is the matter with you, this bright morning?"

Marygold, without taking the apron from her eyes, held out her hand, in which was one of the roses which Midas had so recently transmuted.

"Beautiful!" exclaimed her father. "And what is there in this magnificent golden rose to make you cry?"

"Ah, dear father!" answered the child, as well as her sobs would let her; "it is not beautiful but the ugliest flower that ever grew! As soon as I was dressed I ran into the garden to gather some roses for you. But, oh dear, dear me! What do you think has happened? All the beautiful roses, that smelled so sweetly and had so many lovely blushes, are blighted and spoilt! They are grown quite yellow, as you see this one, and have no longer any fragrance! What can have been the matter?"

"Poh, my dear little girl—pray don't cry about it!" said Midas, who was ashamed to confess that he himself had wrought the change which so greatly afflicted her. "Sit down and eat your bread and milk! You will find it easy enough to exchange a golden rose like that (which will last hundreds of years) for an ordinary one which would wither in a day."

"I don't care for such roses as this!" cried Marygold tossing it contemptuously away. "It has no smell, and the hard petals prick my nose!"

The child now sat down to table, but so occupied with her grief for the blighted roses that she did not even notice the wonderful transmutation of her china bowl. Perhaps this was all the better; for Marygold was accustomed to take pleasure in looking at the queer figures, and strange trees and houses, that were painted on the circumference of the bowl; and these ornaments were now entirely lost in the yellow hue of the metal.

Midas, meanwhile, had poured out a cup of coffee, and, as a matter of course, the coffee-pot, whatever metal it may have been when he took it up, was gold when he set it down. He thought to himself that it was rather an extravagant style of splendor in a king of his simple habits, to breakfast off a service of gold, and began to be puzzled with the difficulty of keeping his treasures safe. Amid these thoughts, he lifted a spoonful of coffee to his lips, and sipping it, was astonished to perceive that, the instant his lips touched the liquid, it became molten gold, and the next moment, hardened into a lump!

"Ha!" exclaimed Midas, rather aghast.

"What is the matter, father?" asked little Marygold, gazing at him, with the tears still standing in her eyes.

"Nothing, child, nothing!" said Midas. "Eat your milk, before it gets quite cold."

He took one of the nice little trouts on his plate, and, by way of experiment, touched its tail with his finger. To his horror, it was immediately transmuted from an admirably fried brook trout into a gold-fish. Its little bones were now golden wires; its fins and tail were thin plates of gold; and there were the marks of the fork in it, and all the delicate, frothy appearance of a nicely fried fish, exactly imitated in metal. A very pretty piece of work, as you may suppose; only King Midas, just at that moment, would much rather have had a real trout in his dish than this elaborate and valuable imitation of one.

"I don't quite see," thought he to himself, "how I am to get any breakfast!"

He took one of the smoking-hot cakes, and had scarcely broken it, when, to his cruel mortification, though a moment before it had been of the whitest wheat, it assumed the yellow hue of Indian meal. Almost in despair, he helped himself to a boiled egg, which immediately underwent a change similar to those of the trout and the cake.

"Well, this is a quandary!" thought he, leaning back in his chair, and looking quite enviously at little Marygold, who was now eating her bread and milk with great satisfaction. "Such a costly breakfast before me, and nothing that can be eaten!"

Hoping that, by dint of great dispatch, he might avoid what he now felt to be a considerable inconvenience, King Midas next snatched a hot potato, and attempted to cram it into his mouth, and swallow it in a hurry. But the Golden Touch was too nimble for him. He found his mouth full, not of mealy potato, but of solid metal, which so burnt his tongue that he roared aloud, and, jumping up from the table, began to dance and stamp about the room, both with pain and affright.

"Father, dear father!" cried little Marygold, who was a very affectionate child, "pray what is the matter?"

"Ah, dear child," groaned Midas, dolefully, "I don't know what is to become of your poor father!"

Here was literally the richest breakfast that could be set before a king, and its very richness made it absolutely good for nothing. The poorest laborer, sitting down to his crust of bread and cup of water, was far better off than King Midas. And what was to be done? Already, at breakfast, Midas was excessively hungry. Would he be less so by dinnertime? And how ravenous would be his appetite for supper, which must undoubtedly consist of the same sort of indigestible dishes as those now before him! How many days, think you, would he survive a continuance of this rich fare?

These reflections so troubled wise King Midas, that he began to doubt whether, after all, riches are the one desirable thing in the world, or even the most desirable. But this was only a passing thought. So fascinated was Midas with the glitter of the yellow metal, that he would still have refused to give up the Golden Touch for so paltry a consideration as breakfast.

Nevertheless, so great was his hunger, and the perplexity of his situation, he again groaned aloud, and very grievously too. Our pretty Marygold could endure it no longer. She sat, a moment, gazing at her father, and trying, with all the might of her little wits, to find out what was the matter with him. Then, with a sweet and sorrowful impulse to comfort him, she started from her chair, and running to Midas, threw her arms affectionately about his knees. He bent down and kissed her. He felt that his little daughter's love was worth a thousand times more than he had gained by the Golden Touch.

"My precious, precious Marygold!" cried he.

But Marygold made no answer.

Alas, what had he done. How fatal was the gift which the stranger bestowed! The moment the lips of Midas touched Marygold's forehead, a change had taken place. Her sweet, rosy face, so full of affection as it had been, assumed a glittering yellow color, with yellow tear-drops congealing on her cheeks. Her beautiful brown ringlets took the same tint. Her soft and tender little form grew hard and inflexible within her father's encircling arms. Little Marygold was a human child no longer, but a golden statue!

Yes, there she was, with the questioning look of love, grief, and pity, hardened into her face. It was the prettiest and most woeful sight that ever mortal saw. All the features and tokens of Marygold were there; even the beloved little dimple remained in her golden chin. But, the more perfect was the resemblance, the greater was the father's agony at beholding this golden image, which was all that was left him of a daughter. Now, at last, when it was too late, he felt how infinitely a warm and tender heart that loved him, exceeded in value all the wealth that could be piled up betwixt the earth and sky!

It would be too sad a story, if I were to tell you how Midas, in the fulness of all his gratified desires, began to wring his hands and bemoan himself; and how he could neither bear to look at Marygold, nor yet to look away from her. There was the precious little figure, with a yellow tear-drop on its yellow cheek, and a look so piteous and tender, that it seemed as if that very expression must needs soften the gold, and make it flesh again.

Midas had only to wring his hands, and to wish that he were the poorest man in the wide world, if the loss of all his wealth might bring back the faintest rose-color to his dear child's face.

While he was in this tumult of despair, he suddenly beheld a stranger standing near the door. Midas bent down his head, without speaking; for he recognized the same figure which had appeared to him, the day before, in the treasure-room, and had bestowed on him the Golden Touch. The stranger's countenance still wore a smile, which seemed to shed a yellow luster all about the room.

"Well, friend Midas," said the stranger, "pray how do you succeed with the Golden Touch?"

Midas shook his head.

"I am very miserable," said he.

"Very miserable, indeed!" exclaimed the stranger. "And how happens that? Have I not faithfully kept my promise with you? Have you not everything that your heart desired?"

"Gold is not everything," answered Midas. "And I have lost all that my heart really cared for."

"Ah! So you have made a discovery, since yesterday?" observed the stranger. "Let us see, then. Which of these two things do you think is really worth the most—the gift of the Golden Touch, or one cup of clear, cold water?"

"Oh blessed water!" exclaimed Midas. "I will never moisten my parched throat again!"

"The Golden Touch," continued the stranger, "or a crust of bread?"

"A piece of bread," answered Midas, "is worth all the gold on earth!"

"The Golden Touch," asked the stranger, "or your own little Marygold, warm, soft, and loving as she was an hour ago?"

"O my child, my dear child!" cried poor Midas, wringing

his hands. "I would not have given that one small dimple in her chin for the power of changing this whole big earth into a solid lump of gold!"

"You are wiser than you were, King Midas!" said the stranger, looking seriously at him. "Your own heart, I perceive, has not been entirely changed from flesh to gold. You appear to be still capable of understanding that the commonest things, such as lie within everybody's grasp, are more valuable than the riches which so many mortals sigh and struggle after. Tell me, now, do you sincerely desire to rid yourself of this Golden Touch?"

"It is hateful to me!" replied Midas.

A fly settled on his nose, but immediately fell to the floor, for it, too, had become gold. Midas shuddered.

"Go then," said the stranger, "plunge into the river that glides past the bottom of your garden. Take likewise a vase of the same water, and sprinkle it over any object that you may desire to change back again from gold into its former substance. If you do this in earnestness and sincerity, it may possibly repair the mischief which your avarice has occasioned."

King Midas bowed low; and when he lifted his head, the lustrous stranger had vanished.

You will easily believe that Midas lost no time in snatching up a great earthen pitcher (but, alas me! it was no longer earthen after he touched it), and hastening to the riverside. As he scampered along, and forced his way through the shrubbery, it was positively marvellous to see how the foliage turned yellow behind him, as if the autumn had been there, and nowhere else. On reaching the river's brink, he plunged headlong in, without waiting so much as to pull off his shoes.

"Poof! poof! poof!" snorted King Midas, as his head emerged out of the water. "Well; this is really a refreshing bath, and

I think it must have quite washed away the Golden Touch. And now for filling my pitcher!" As he dipped the pitcher in the water, it gladdened his very heart to see it change from gold into the same good, honest earthen vessel which it had been before he touched it.   He was conscious, also, of a change within himself. A cold, hard, and heavy weight seemed to have gone out of his bosom. Perceiving a violet that grew on the bank of the river, Midas touched it with his finger and was overjoyed to find that the delicate flower retained its purple hue, instead of undergoing a yellow blight. The curse of the Golden Touch had really been removed from him.

King Midas hastened back to the palace. The first thing he did was to sprinkle water over the golden figure of little Marygold.

You would have laughed to see how she began to sneeze and sputter! How astonished she was to find herself dripping wet, and her father still throwing more water over her! For Marygold did not know that she had been a little golden statue, nor could she remember anything that had happened since the moment when she ran with out-stretched arms to comfort poor King Midas.

Her father led her into the garden where he sprinkled all the remainder of the water over the rosebushes, and five-thousand roses recovered their beautiful bloom. There were two circumstances, however, which as long as he lived, used to put King Midas in mind of the Golden Touch. One was that the sands of the river sparkled like gold. The other, that little Marygold's hair had now a golden tinge which he had never observed.

When King Midas had grown quite an old man and trotted Marygold's children on his knee, he was fond of telling them this story. And then would he stroke their glossy ringlets and tell them that their hair, likewise, had a rich shade of gold.

"And to tell you the truth," quoth King Midas, diligently trotting the children all the while, "ever since that morning, I have hated the very sight of all other gold, save this!"